BOOTS & BAREBACK

UGLY STICK SALOON SERIES #5

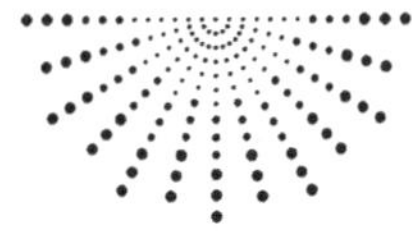

MYLA JACKSON

TWISTED PAGE INC

EBOOK ISBN: 978-1-62695-096-2

PRINT ISBN: 978-1-62695-097-9

I dedicate this book to those wonderful bars in the big and small towns where people go to connect with others and find more there than they imagined possible. Mechanical bulls, guys who'll actually dance, cowboys, cowgirls, friends and lovers. A place where everyone knows your name.

I'd also like to thank my readers for being so loyal to the Ugly Stick Saloon. As a gift to you, I've included BOOTS & PROMISES in this print version. Happy Reading!
Elle James

BOOTS & PROMISES

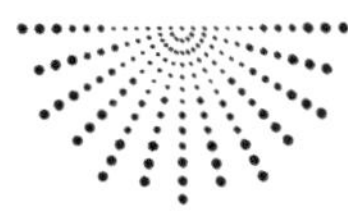

UGLY STICK SALOON SERIES BOOK #4

New York Times & USA Today
Bestselling Author

ELLE JAMES

writing as

MYLA JACKSON

BOOTS & PROMISES

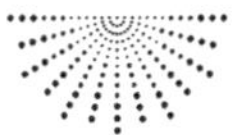

*E*lla Lang stood in the bedroom doorway of her tiny Manhattan apartment, staring at the man she loved more than life.

Jesse James O'Brien lay spread out naked across the sheets. Six feet three inches of muscled cowboy, his feet hanging over the end of the double bed, the most gorgeous specimen of masculinity a woman could ever hope for.

The night had been grueling at the theater. Nothing had gone right. Stage props hadn't cooperated. Ella had not one, but three, wardrobe malfunctions and missed one of her cues.

Her focus hadn't been on her performance, so much as on this man, this fish-out-of-water cowboy who had no business moving to New York just because she had.

Hindsight being twenty-twenty, Ella knew she should never have let him come. He belonged in Texas on the Rockin' O Ranch with his father and brothers and sister, not cooped up in a postage-stamp apartment, searching for work in a city that preferred celebrities over honest, hard-working cowboys.

God, he looked so peaceful, lying sprawled across the bed.

Ella didn't want to wake him. Instead, she eased around the corner of the bed and entered the tiny bathroom, peeled off her clothes and showered away the residual stage makeup and hairspray that was as much a part of a performer's life as her voice and acting. She towel-dried her hair and debated slipping into a nightgown or just sleeping naked like Jesse. After only a moment's hesitation, her pussy growing warm and wet, she opted for naked. She hung the towel on the towel bar and turned to switch off the light. At that moment, she noticed the blue jeans hanging on a hook on the back of the bathroom door.

Jesse's jeans.

She lifted them down and hugged them to her chest, the scent of Jesse and denim reminding her of Texas and the home she'd left to follow her dreams. Visions of wide-open spaces and fields of fresh green hay came to mind, kicking her in the gut with a truckload of homesickness. Refusing to give into the ready tears building in her eyes, Ella folded the jeans over her arm, intent on hanging them in the closet in the bedroom.

Something dropped from one of the pockets and bounced off her foot, causing her to glance down. On the floor beside her lay a tiny box.

Heart thumping, Ella bent to retrieve it, her knees nearly giving way as she realized what it was. The little blue package with a pretty white bow had bold black letters spelling *Tiffany & Co* written in neat script across the top.

Ella's heartbeat skittered to a halt and her hand shook so badly she dropped the box again. This time, as she lifted it, she couldn't resist. She had to see what was inside. She pressed an ear to the door. No sounds emanated from the other side as Jesse slept on.

After slipping the bow off the edge, she removed the box lid. Inside was a black ring box. She lifted it from the blue packaging and pushed open the lid. Nestled against midnight-black velvet was a breathtakingly beautiful, marquis-shaped diamond on a simple white-gold band.

Her breath caught, joy filling her heart so full her chest hurt.

Jesse was going to ask her to marry him. As the reality and enormity of what he was about to do sank in, she sat down hard on the floor, the tiles cool against her naked bottom. The cold against her skin spread quickly, shadowing the initial joy.

Ella had waited so long for Jesse to ask her to marry him. Before she landed a significant role on Broadway, she wouldn't have thought twice about giving up all her dreams to get hitched and stay in Texas, raising horses and babies. Now...she had too much invested in NYC. She couldn't go back. Not yet. Part of her would regret not fulfilling her life's ambitions, always wondering if she'd made the right decision, never seeing her name, Ella Lang, on a playbill or in neon lights across a marquee.

If this ring was what she thought it was, Jesse was going to ask her to marry him. And he'd probably insist on staying in this metropolis that, as far as Ella could tell, had been nothing but a disappointment to the Texas cowboy.

Ella closed the box and held it to her aching breast. She now knew what she had to do. She couldn't let Jesse make this big of a mistake. She loved him too much to let him sacrifice all his own dreams and desires just to be with her. He deserved to find someone who would happily live on the ranch and help him raise cows and horses...and babies.

She gulped, swallowing back a wave of longing so strong it nearly made her moan.

Jesse needed a woman who didn't long for a career in the performance arts and had to live in a metropolis the size of New York City or Los Angeles to fulfill her dream.

Her heart breaking into a million pieces, Ella tucked the ring box back in his jeans and hung them exactly the way she'd found them on the back of the door. Her chest hurt so badly she could barely breathe past her constricted vocal chords.

Careful not to disturb Jesse, she slipped into bedroom and onto the bed, wanting only to get as close to him as possible.

As she lay on her side, facing away from the man she cared so much about, she fought back tears. Ella didn't want him to see them. Didn't want him to know how much she would hurt to say what she had to say.

He rolled over, his body spooning hers, warming her backside.

Ella wanted so badly to turn toward him and hold him, make love to him, have him drive deep inside her. He was her soul-mate, her love, her entire life. She couldn't imagine loving any other man. Ever. Nor could she imagine life without him.

But she had to.

Jesse had given up everything he'd loved to follow her to New York, claiming he could make the situation work. He was smart, hard-working and educated, but, as far as Ella could gather, no matter how many doors he'd knocked on in the big Apple, he had yet to find work that suited him.

But then what work was there in NYC for a man born, bred and raised a cowboy from a long line of ranchers in West Texas? The man had cattle and horses in his blood. He loved the wide-open spaces and working with animals.

Yet, when Ella had chosen to follow her dream to perform on Broadway, he'd followed.

Tears welled and a giant lump formed in her throat, making breathing difficult . Had she been too selfish? All her life she'd trained to be a performer—dance classes, acting lessons, a degree in drama from Julliard. She'd worked too hard to give up her dream. Now that she'd gotten her break, she had to take advantage while she was still young and pretty enough to make an impression on a casting director.

Jesse had been a very supportive lover. He'd driven her to the airport when she'd left for NYC for weeks at a time, suffering through her disappointments and the endless auditions, even coming along on several occasions.

Now that Ella was realizing her dream, Jesse had

chosen to join her in NYC permanently. He couldn't live without her, he'd said.

But Ella knew Jesse. For two months he hadn't said a word about Texas, his horse, Paddy, or his close-knit family. He'd claimed being on his own would be a refreshing break , without his brothers and sister constantly interfering in his life. NYC would be an adventure.

While Ella spent her days practicing for the show, her nights performing, Jesse was left on his own to find work, clean the apartment or watch television. He'd never faltered in his commitment to be with her, never said anything about his disappointment on the employment front. As far as Ella could tell, he hadn't found anything, but he'd spend every day out of the apartment. *Working on his plan*, he'd insisted.

God, she loved him…

That's why she couldn't marry him, couldn't even let him ask. She'd be too tempted to say yes. He'd never be happy in a city, away from his family and his beloved ranch and horses. Texas was as much a part of him as breathing.

Ella had her work, the stage, everything she'd worked for.

Jesse's hand slipped up over her hip to cup one of her breasts and he stirred against her, his cock nudging her bottom. "Hey darlin'," he said in his slow southern drawl that melted Ella every time he spoke. "Whatcha thinkin'?"

She swallowed the lump knotting in her throat. "How much I wanted you to wake up and make love to me."

His chuckle rumbled in his chest, vibrating against her

back, his breath stirring the tendrils of hair on the back of Ella's neck. "Hmmm. I don't know if I have it in me," he said.

Ella scooted backward, fitting his shaft into the crease between her butt cheeks. "I think you have the right equipment for the job. I suppose you don't have the right motivation."

His fingers squeezed the tip of her nipple. "What kind of motivation do you propose?"

She grabbed a condom from the ready stash on her nightstand, rolled over to straddle him and planted her knees on either side of his hips. "Is this more inspiring?"

Jesse smiled up at Ella, as she tore open the packet and removed the rubber.

With her hands poised to slip the condom down over his stiff, hard member, she couldn't help thinking this might be the last time, and her heart clenched.

Jesse caught her hands. "Darlin', I've been thinking… we need to talk."

Ella laughed, the sound more of a sob. She couldn't let him declare his love one more time. The pain would be more than she could bear. "Don't talk, just love me." She shook off his grip, slid her ass down his legs and took his long, thick length into her mouth. Cupping his balls, she massaged them between her fingers.

His eyes closed and he breathed deeply, his chest rising and falling, his hips lifting beneath her, pressing deeper until he bumped against the back of her throat. "Really, Ella, we should talk."

She worked his scrotum, her fingers squeezing, releasing. Her mouth slid up his cock, her tongue swirling around the head, catching the bulbous rim. Ella stuck the tip of her tongue in the hole, tasting his pre-come, her own body awash with heat. "You really want to talk when we could fuck?" she said around his hard dick.

"Baby, you know I can't resist when you talk dirty."

"Then ride me, cowboy." Her throat tightened but she forced the words past the lump. "Ride me like there's no tomorrow."

He bucked beneath her, shoving back into her mouth, his hips driving upward, over and over.

She could feel his body tensing, his cock increasing in size and thickness until the shaft was so hard, it had to hurt.

Then he pulled Ella off, laying her down beside him. "You first."

"No, it's okay, really," she protested, afraid she'd lose control of her emotions if he was too nice. "I love it when you come first."

He pressed a finger to her lips and replaced it with his mouth, his tongue thrusting inside, swirling around hers while his hands cupped her face, holding her as if she was something precious.

Jesse always made Ella feel like the center of his universe. She swallowed a wave of tears lumping in her throat.

His mouth shifted off her lips and slid over her chin, maneuvering a path downward along the long line of her neck, stopping to test her pulse at the base of her throat.

Without too much pause, he continued to her distended nipples, taking one between his teeth, biting down gently, tugging at the turgid peak until Ella's back arched off the bed, pushing more of her breast into his mouth.

He leaned to the side, a hand slipping over her ribs, past her bellybutton to the thatch of hair covering her pussy.

Ella's belly tightened, her thighs twitching, her core aching for more of Jesse. "Please," she begged.

"Please what?" he asked, his breath blowing over her dampened nipple.

"Enough foreplay, fuck me already."

He shook his head, his fingers stroking the curly hairs at the apex of her thighs like a man would stroke the fur of a kitten. "Patience, little one." He bent to take the other nipple between his lips, sucking it fully into his mouth, pulling hard as his fingers slipped between her slick folds.

Ella raised her knees, digging her heels into the mattress, sharp tingling sensations starting in her toes and spreading upward.

He knew what she liked—slow steady strokes, his fingers dipping lower, pushing into her pussy for the lubricating moisture of her juices. Then he slid back to the nubbin of skin that contained a myriad of nerve endings, each twitching, firing off electric pulses.

Ella reached down to cup his hand, shoving it lower to push his fingers deep into her cunt. She writhed beneath him, soon too frustrated with the fingers and eager for his full, thick cock.

"Fuck me now, cowboy," she cried, squirming beneath him, her fingers threading through his hair, pulling him upward.

He held his ground, refusing to rise to her demand. "Not until you're there."

"I'm so close, so very close." And she wanted that most intimate of connections, with him driving deep inside her, filling all the places that would soon be empty. A sob rose up her throat, threatening to chill her arousal.

"Then you only need a little more of this." With the tip of his finger drenched in her come, he flicked her clit, starting slow and building up speed until the tingling in her toes became all-consuming explosions of her senses throughout her body.

Her back arched off the bed. Ella grabbed his hand and held it still as she catapulted over the edge, her body jerking with the orgasm's intensity.

He took the condom from her nerveless fingers, slipped it over his dick in a quick, sure movement, one he'd done so many times before in the months they'd been living together.

Heat continued to surge low in her belly, her pussy drenched in lubricating come.

Jesse rose to his knees, turned her over and brought her up on all fours and then plunged in, riding her like a bronco buster at a rodeo, slapping her ass just the way she liked. He stiffened, his hands on her hips gripping so hard, his fingers dug into her flesh. One final thrust and he pulled free. "Oh God, Ella, I don't think I'll ever get enough of you," he said on a sigh.

He collapsed on the bed, his arms wrapping around her.

Ella snuggled close, drinking in the beauty of him, the

strength and kindness, the raw sexual machine. She wanted to remember every detail.

For a few long minutes, they lay in each other's arms, body heat cooling, breathing returning to normal.

Ella relaxed against him, pushing to the back of her mind that their time together was limited.

Jesse smoothed a strand of hair out of her face. "Ella, we need to talk."

"Did you hear from home today?" she asked, hoping to sidetrack him from asking her *the* question, postponing it long enough for her to convince him to go back to Texas.

He smiled. "Talked to Gabe, today."

"How're your brothers and sister?"

"Missing us, but fine."

Her heart skipped several beats as she contemplated her next words. "Jesse, that brings up a good point."

"Yes, it does," he agreed.

Ella gulped air and jumped in. "Good. Then you agree, you should go home."

"What?" He leaned back enough to stare into her eyes. "Where did that thought come from?"

"I've been thinking..."

Jesse smiled. "Female thinking?"

She shrugged. He liked to tease her about some of her ideas, especially when it came to reading his mind. Which she could rarely do. "I work a lot and we rarely see each other. Plus, you've been here for two months and have yet to find any job that suits you." She touched a hand to the side of his face, her breath tight in her chest. "It's not fair for me to want to keep you here. Texas is your home."

He captured her hand in his and turned up her palm,

pressing a kiss inside. "I want to be here with you. I've been working on something. I'm sure it'll come through soon. Just you wait and see." He gave her a half-smile, his eyes twinkling. "I love you, Ella."

She closed her eyes, knowing what she had to do and that task wasn't going to be easy. Not when she loved him so much. "Jesse, I need to concentrate on my work. If I want to make it as a performer, I can't be tied down, worrying about someone else. I need to be free to come and go, without concern for another person. I can't do that with you here. You need to go home." She forced out the words with as much conviction as she could instill without breaking down and sobbing.

Jesse's brows furrowed. "Are you telling me that what we have between us means nothing to you?"

She could see the hurt in his chocolate brown eyes and hated herself for lying to him, even if doing so was for his own good. Ella shook her head, tears welling in her eyes, but she refused to let them fall. She had to keep up the pretense long enough to convince Jesse he wasn't wanted in New York City anymore. "I'll always love you, but now just isn't the right time for us. I have to work long hours, you can't find work and, you said so yourself, your family misses you. I want you to go back to Texas where you belong. You should leave tomorrow."

"I thought I belonged with you." A broad fingertip brushed hair over her ear. "The job situation will work itself out. I'll find something sooner than you think."

"No, Jesse. You don't fit in here. You're a cowboy, used to wide-open countryside and working with the horses and cattle. You don't belong here."

His frown deepened. "I told you, I'll make it work."

"You shouldn't have to. You *belong* in Texas. I know you miss your family and your horse." She leaned her forehead on his chest, her heart hurting so badly, she thought it would stop.

"I love you more than my horse, Ella." He pulled her close, his arms like iron bands.

She wanted him to hold her forever, forget all she'd said and just love her. "Tomorrow," she whispered and looked up at him through tear-filled eyes.

He stared, his mouth opened then closed. "Are you sure that's how you want it?"

Ella nodded, unable to speak at that point, afraid if she opened her mouth, she'd break into sobs, taking back everything she'd said.

"Can I at least think about it and give you my answer tomorrow?"

Ella didn't think she could take another conversation like this one, but she nodded.

"Is it okay if I stay tonight and hold you one last time?" he whispered into her hair.

Her arms circled his waist, and she hugged him close, her eyes dry, her heart in ruins. She'd just asked the only man she ever loved to leave. How would she go on in this big, lonely city full of strangers without her cowboy?

FOR THE REST of the night, she lay in his arms, afraid to sleep and miss even a moment more with Jesse. When morning dawned, Ella had to get up and go to rehearsal.

Jesse rose before her and had breakfast waiting on the

tiny dinette table. He didn't meet her gaze, his face, dark and brooding.

When the time came to leave, her hand froze on the doorknob. She couldn't twist it.

Jesse stepped up behind her and gripped her shoulders, turning her in his arms. Then with the familiar tenderness he always showed, he kissed her, his lips moving over hers as if she was a delicate flower whose petals he could only sip from. His arms circled Ella's waist and he crushed her to his chest.

Ella clung to him, her breathing ragged, sobs rising up her throat.

After a long moment, he tipped up her chin. "Meet me at the corner of Central Park South and 5th Avenue at noon, during your lunch break."

She stared at him, searching for a clue in his expression, reluctant to commit.

He shook her arms gently. "Promise?"

Afraid she'd fall apart, Ella could only nod. Then she tore herself away and ran through the door without looking back.

THAT DAY AT REHEARSAL, she stumbled, forgot lines, and cried when she should have laughed.

The director threw the script at her and called for a two-hour lunch break. "Come back with your head screwed on straight, or don't come back at all."

Mortified, Ella slinked away from the theater, sure she'd be fired by the end of the day and not caring one bit. After walking for several blocks, she realized she'd lost the most important person in her life and beyond that, acting was so inconsequential it didn't matter anymore. At that point she began to run. Only the distance was too far to run all the way to Central Park and make it by noon.

Racing to the corner, Ella tried waving down a taxi, but every last one was full. Frantic now, she stepped in front of a bicycle courier and almost made him wreck.

"I'll give you..." She dug in her pocket for her last two twenties. "Forty dollars to get me to Central Park by noon."

His lips turned down into a grimace. "Are you crazy? It's already eleven fifty-five. I'd barely make it riding alone."

She held up the bills. "Forty bucks says you can get me there."

The cyclist hesitated, staring at the two twenties. After ten agonizing seconds, he scooted down off his seat and jerked his head backward. "You can have the seat. Hold on tight, I'll be making some tight corners."

Ella jumped on, wrapped her arms around his skinny waist and prayed as he pushed out into the insane Manhattan traffic.

The courier pumped the pedals like a maniac, his body rising and falling, his weight adding thrust to their forward motion. Soon they were zipping between stalled taxis stuck in gridlock, bumped up on sidewalks when they had to, and narrowly missed being struck by vehicles running red lights. Horns honked, drivers cursed and breath lodged tight in her chest, Ella saw her life pass before her eyes more times than she cared to count.

At noon, they crossed Central Park South, wove through the pedestrians and stopped at Grand Army Plaza. Ella cursed the bright sunny day that brought New Yorkers out by the thousands for a chance to escape their dreary offices. How was she supposed to find Jesse in the crowd?

The courier snatched the twenties she held out and kicked off, heading back in the direction he'd come, claiming he was late for a delivery.

Ella glanced at her watch. She'd missed the time by five minutes. Would he have waited or decided she wasn't coming and left?

After pushing her way through the crowd on either side of the corner for half a block, Ella worked her way back to lean against the base of the golden statue of General Sherman, her hopes diminishing by the second, her heart breaking into a thousand pieces. She didn't have time now to go back to their apartment and check for him there. Her feet dragged along the concrete. She'd miss afternoon practice all together.

So?

Ella straightened and was about to run toward the street and throw herself in front of a taxi when a stir in the crowd captured her attention. People stopped and pointed toward the park behind her, their eyes round, smiles lighting their faces.

Though in a hurry, she chanced a quick glance over her shoulder and ground to a halt.

Four mounted patrolmen approached on horseback. They stopped within twenty feet of Ella, leaving space for a fifth rider to pass between.

Riding a dappled gray gelding that looked suspiciously like Paddy and wearing the navy blue uniform of a New York City police officer, Jesse James O'Brien pulled off his helmet as he reined in his mount.

Ella couldn't catch her breath. Her heart skipped several beats then settled into a rapid, raucous rhythm, and she thought she might hyperventilate. "Jesse?"

He smiled, dismounted and closed the distance between them. He didn't touch her or hold her.

Every fiber of Ella's being wanted to throw herself into his arms and call herself every kind of fool for telling him to go home, but all she could do was stand there and stare. In a uniform or jeans and cowboy hat, he was the most handsome man she'd ever met.

"What's all this?" she asked, her words coming out in a breathless squeak. She waved at his uniform and the other men on horseback.

"Last night I tried to tell you, but you seemed hell bent on sending me away, instead." His shoulders straightened and he stood tall. "I found a job."

"You did?" Her words were short, breathy. "How? When?"

"I'd been working on it for weeks. Did I mention I have family here in New York City?"

Ella nodded, vaguely remembering he'd come from a long line of Irish immigrants who'd landed on Ellis Island.

"They helped me get an interview and start my training. This," he waved at the uniform and Paddy, "is only temporary until I complete all the requirements. But I wanted this day to be special, so they helped me out."

Ella touched the dappled gray's nose. "How did you get Paddy here?"

Jesse grinned. "Gabe brought him all the way from Texas." He looked back over his shoulder and waved.

Gabe O'Brien stepped out from beneath the shadow of a tree and lifted a hand.

Too stunned to speak, Ella shook her head.

"I was waiting for Paddy to arrive." Jesse reached out and held her hand. "I wanted to surprise you."

"But why all the secrecy?"

He chuckled. "I knew you thought I couldn't fit in, but I wanted to have proof, to show you that I could. I have family and I have my horse and a job." He dropped down on one knee. "The only thing I don't have is you." He pulled the little blue box from his pocket and held it out. "If you still don't want me to go home, would you consider marrying this New York City cowboy and putting him out of his misery? I've missed you for five long hours. I don't know if I can go another five minutes without knowing you're in my life. Will you be my wife?"

A sigh rose from the crowd that had gathered around the horses and police officers.

"Say yes!" a woman shouted.

"Say yes!" called another woman.

Before long, everyone standing in the vicinity chanted *Yes! Yes! Yes!*

Tears streaked down Ella's face, and she kneeled and flung her arms around Jesse's neck. "I thought I'd lost you." She hiccoughed and cried. "I don't care if I ever perform on Broadway again. I'd go back to Texas today, if you wanted me to."

"Baby, I want you to stay here." He pulled her into his arms and held her tight. "You have a gift. I wouldn't ever ask you to give it up."

"But what about home...Texas.?" She buried her face in his neck, her tears staining his crisp blue collar.

"My home is with you, wherever we are."

"Hey lady, my lunch break is almost over. Would ya say yes already?" a dark-haired, and somewhat harried, woman stood over Ella and Jesse, her arms crossed over her chest, her brows narrowed.

Ella laughed and hugged Jesse around the neck then raised her voice for all to hear, "Yes!"

A cheer went up, startling the horses. Paddy stamped his feet.

Jesse rose, bringing her with him, his arm around her waist. "I love you, Ella."

"You're my one, my only...and you are truly amazing." Ella flung her arms around his neck and kissed him. "I love my New York City cowboy."

BOOTS & BAREBACK

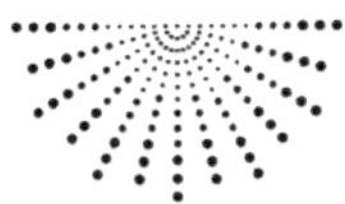

UGLY STICK SALOON SERIES #5

New York Times & USA Today
Bestselling Author

ELLE JAMES

writing as

MYLA JACKSON

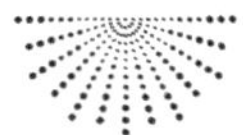

"Well, I reckon it'll do for a bachelor party. Mind if your old man comes along for a beer?" Jonathon O'Brien, owner of the Rockin' O Ranch hadn't seen the inside of the Ugly Stick Saloon for a couple years. He hadn't felt much like getting out since his wife had died of breast cancer.

"What's not to love about this place?" Gabe, Jonathon's oldest son, waved a hand at the crowded interior of the Ugly Stick. "It's got atmosphere."

"They can provide the whiskey and stripper," Tanner, the second oldest, noted. "That's all we need."

"Don't be such an ass." Sean elbowed his older brother.

"Why's that being as ass?" Tanner frowned. "So I like women. The nakeder the better. And that makes me an ass? I don't see you turning down the fairer sex."

"Point made." Sean chuckled. "But you're still an ass."

Tanner punched his brother in the arm. "Yeah, but you're my brother. Takes one to know one."

"Can you quit jackin' around and focus?" Gabe interceded. "We're here to commission this place for our little brother's bachelor party."

Jonathon shook his head, staring around the table at three of his four sons, his only daughter around the joint somewhere, waiting tables. "I can't get over it. Of all my children, my youngest son's going to be the first to get hitched." He frowned at his grown sons, ranging in age from twenty-seven to thirty-one. "What are the rest of you waiting for?"

Gabe, Tanner and Sean's eyes widened and they stared at each other.

Gabe raised a hand. "Now, Dad, don't start."

"Start what?" Jonathon waved a hand around the room. "There are plenty of nice young women around these parts, many of which would be happy to marry into the O'Brien family." Each of his sons stood to inherit large parcels of land when he died. What woman wouldn't want to be a part of that? "You've all proven yourselves good ranchers, increasing the size of our herd, building our stock of working and racing horses. And you've each done good at your other interests. You're all strong and good-looking men, even if I *am* a little biased. 'Course you look like your old man." He puffed out his chest and grinned. "Okay, better, but then I have a few years on you."

"Dad…" Tanner shook his head. "We've been over this. We'll get married."

"Someday," Gabe added.

"When we find the right woman," Sean finished.

A dark-haired beauty passed by, carrying a tray loaded

with beer mugs and whiskey shooters. A rowdy cowboy reached out and pinched her ass.

She turned, her cheeks bright pink, and slapped the man in the face, almost spilling the tray of drinks. "Keep your hands to yourself, George."

Jonathon chuckled, liking that she was embarrassed by the unwanted advance, but that she could stand up for herself. She reminded him of his dearly departed wife when she was about that age. "What about her?"

"Isabella?" Gabe asked, his eyes narrowing. "She's pretty, all right. But I've asked and she refuses to go out with me."

"Really?" Sean grinned. "I asked her too, and got the same brush-off."

Tanner's gaze followed Isabella as she wove through the tables. "Apparently, she doesn't care for the O'Briens."

Gabe clapped his brother on the back. "Turned you down too, did she?"

"I didn't say that." Tanner glowered at Gabe.

Jonathon chewed on a toothpick, studying the gal in question. "Got good hips. Would bear children well."

Gabe shook his head. "Dad, we aren't looking for breeding stock."

"She's got nice—" Sean made the universal motion for figure until Tanner planted his elbow in his belly.

"Don't be so coarse." Tanner's brows rose. "Isabella's a nice girl. That's probably why she won't go out with you."

"Did any of you ask her more than once?" Jonathon demanded.

"After she turned me down flat, I didn't see the point." Gabe scratched the five-o'clock shadow on his chin. "Still don't know why she wouldn't even go out for a cup of coffee."

"You were shit-faced drunk. That's why." Tanner lifted his mug and emptied the last swallow. "Point is, Dad, I haven't found the right woman."

"I kinda thought Isabella was that woman. She's not like any of the others." Sean stared after Isabella as she returned to the bar with a tray of empties and orders for more drinks.

"Yeah, she's got a great laugh when you can get her to loosen up." Gabe's gaze followed Isabella as well. "But you can't make someone love you."

"Are any of you even trying to find a woman?" Jonathan glanced at each of his sons, one at a time.

Tanner frowned. "Dad, it's not like shopping. You can't just choose one off the shelf."

"You have to be persistent and let a gal know you're serious." Jonathon smacked his palm on the table. "I want grandchildren. Lots of them. You can't be too picky or all the good ones'll be gone before you know it."

"And how long did it take you to find Mom?" Sean asked.

Jonathon's head rose, his chest swelling. "I fell in love with your mother the first time I saw her. I knew by the second date I was gonna ask her to marry me."

Isabella stopped at their table and collected the empties. When she smiled, all three of Jonathon's sons smiled back. Damned if they weren't taken with this little girl.

"Can I get you boys anything?" she asked.

"Well, as a matter of fact…" Jonathon started.

"Dad…" Gabe warned. "She's asking about drinks."

Jonathon frowned at his oldest son. "I'd like to talk to the owner."

"And we'd like another round." Tanner drew a circle with his finger over the table.

"I'll be back in a minute." Isabella turned, her long, rich, brown hair swinging over her shoulders, and her short, frayed cutoffs barely covering the curve of her ass.

"Yeah, I think she'll do," Jonathon muttered, an idea spinning in his head. "Is Isabella one of the for-hire strippers?"

"I don't think so." Gabe glanced at the dance floor, his boot tapping to the beat of the music. "Why don't you ask her when she comes back?"

"I will." It was about time someone did something about getting his sons married off. Since the three at the table didn't seem to be in any hurry, it was time he took matters in his own hands. "You say a woman owns this place now?" Curious about the owner, Jonathon craned his neck, searching the interior of the saloon for an older female face that looked like she'd be the owner.

"That's right." Tanner nodded toward the strawberry-blonde beauty behind the bar, helping out. "Audrey Anderson bought it."

"The pretty blonde? Is she old enough to serve whiskey?" Jonathon scratched his head.

Gabe laughed. "She's almost my age, Dad. And she's pretty smart."

"Why don't one of you go out with her?"

"She's taken." Tanner crooked his head toward the tall, dark-skinned Kiowa cowboy leaning on the bar. "Jackson

Gray Wolf staked his claim and they seem plenty happy. Wouldn't be surprised to hear wedding bells soon."

"That's what I mean." Jonathon's lips twisted. "If you boys take too long deciding which girl is right for you, you'll miss out on all the good ones."

"Well, hell, Dad, I'd better get out on that dance floor and find me a woman before they get snatched up." Tanner pushed back his chair and stood, cracking his knuckles. "Lemme see. That pretty redhead oughta do." He struck out across the floor for the bar. Before he got there, another man stepped up to the redhead, said something that made her smile and led her out on the dance floor.

Gabe chuckled across the table. "Seems our brother missed his shot at another one of the good ones."

"See what I mean?" Jonathon crossed his arms.

Tanner moved to the brunette who'd been sitting next to the redhead. She shook her head and held up her hand, flashing a wedding ring.

After one more try, Tanner returned to the table, a scowl marring his tanned brow. "Didn't really feel like dancin' anyway. Besides, I think the show is about to start."

Isabella returned with a tray of drinks, plunking them on the wooden tabletop, one at a time.

Jonathon leaned toward her as she passed by him. She even smelled pretty. Yup, if she was willing and the creek didn't rise, he'd hire her to perform at the bachelor party. Maybe that would get the ball rolling.

Audrey Anderson moved in behind Isabella. "I'll take

that tray. You'd better get into your costume for the show."

Jonathon's ears perked. "She's in the show?"

"All my girls either sing or dance as part of their duties at the Ugly Stick Saloon." Audrey smiled at Isabella's retreating figure. "And we have a special presentation tonight. A new toy I've added to the Ugly Stick arsenal and hopefully a way for the girls to earn a few more tips." Audrey winked.

"What is it?" Sean leaned forward.

"You'll see." She nodded toward the stage where all three of the Gray Wolf brothers were pushing a big machine out onto the dance floor.

Tanner's frown lightened. "Is that a mechanical bull?"

"Close." Audrey grinned. "It's a mechanical horse. The only one of its kind, as far as I know."

"I've never seen one before. I thought mechanical bulls went out in the seventies." Jonathan had ridden a few mechanical bulls in his younger days. "They never did give the same look and feel of riding the rodeo circuit, but they were good for training and impressing the gals."

"I found this one at an auction and had it repainted and tuned up." She clapped her hands and glanced at the chair beside Jonathon. "Mind if I join you? Isabella is up first and I didn't get to see her practice."

Jonathon jumped up and pulled the chair out for her. "Please. I have something I want to talk to you about after the show."

Audrey dropped into the chair, turning to face the dance floor. "Isabella really didn't want to be the first to perform on the horse in public, but I insisted. She's the best rider we have."

"Why didn't she want to do it?"

"She doesn't think she's sexy enough to pull it off." Audrey snorted. "That girl just needs to look in a mirror."

Jonathon agreed and his sons apparently did too.

Gabe, Sean and Tanner craned their necks, waiting for Isabella to appear.

Jonathon wanted to see Isabella in action as well, before he committed to hiring her for the bachelor party. Although he'd pretty much decided on her anyway. She was pretty, sexy and could take care of herself.

The band struck up the tune to some country song about saving horses and riding cowboys.

From the back of the bar behind the stage, Isabella emerged wearing black leather chaps, black cowboy boots with rhinestone studs and a bright red bikini. Nothing else.

"Hot damn, that outfit makes me horny." Audrey sat forward and hooted along with the rest of the crowd. "Not sexy, my ass. Isabella's hot tonight!"

Isabella's gaze remained fixed on the mechanical horse. She placed her boots one in front of the other as she walked through the throng of cowboys. When she reached the horse, Jackson Gray Wolf grabbed her around the middle and swung her up on the fiberglass body.

"That horse doesn't have a saddle. How's she going to stay on?" Jonathon asked.

"Isabella assured me she was used to riding bareback." Audrey leaned toward Gabe, her eyelids drooping. In a conspiratorial whisper, loud enough for all at the table to hear, she added, "She told me she prefers to ride bareback in the moonlight, but this will have to do."

Jonathon shot a glance at Gabe, Tanner and Sean. Each of his sons' gazes followed the woman up onto the horse, where she straddled the beast, wrapping her legs around its middle. She gave Jackson a nod and he reached to push the On switch.

The horse lurched forward.

Isabella kept her seat, her back straight, her legs tightening around the fiberglass body.

As the music swelled, the horse settled into a smooth and easy rocking motion.

Isabella swayed with the electronic creature, her movements all sex-in-motion.

When the horse spun to the side, she stayed with it, her body twisting and bending in a languid, captivating style.

Jonathon alternated between watching the girl and watching his sons. When the song came to an end, men were tossing twenties at the base of the contraption, yelling for an encore. Gabe rose, his hand going to his pocket. Tanner and Sean followed suit, each reaching for their wallets.

Jonathon grinned. "Yessirree, she's the one."

Smiling broadly, Audrey turned to Jonathon. "I'm sorry, did you say something?"

"Miss Anderson, I have a proposition for you."

She winked, her smile broadening. "Now, Mr. O'Brien, I'll take that as a compliment, however, my man might not." She tossed her hair, motioning toward Jackson who was standing guard beside the mechanical horse and its sin-worthy rider.

"Not that I wouldn't be tempted by such a lovely lady, but I'd like to hire your establishment for my son's bachelor party."

"Now *that* I can do." She turned to face him. "When are you planning this event and what kind of food and entertainment would you like to provide for your guests?"

"A week from today, I'll leave the food up to you, and I want her." He pointed to the woman on the fake horse. "Is she one of your for-hire strippers?"

Audrey frowned. "No, Isabella made it clear she doesn't want to hire out as a stripper. She doesn't think she's as pretty or sexy as the other girls."

"Seriously?"

"She has confidence issues where her sexuality is concerned. I don't get it, but she does. How about Lacey?" Audrey pointed toward one of the women holding a full tray of beverages, fielding passes from every man at the table she was serving. "Lacey's one of my best and she's sexy as hell."

"Nope." Jonathon nodded toward Isabella and made his stand. "We want her. If you can't get her, the deal's off."

The owner of the Ugly Stick Saloon stared across the floor at Isabella. "She's a beauty, but she's never expressed an interest in stripping." Audrey shrugged. "All I can do is ask."

"Tell her I'll pay her five hundred dollars a dance if she'll do it. And I'll pay you a thousand-dollar commission to get her to agree, on top of renting the saloon for the party." He pulled his wallet out, extracted ten one-hundred-dollar bills and slapped them on the table. "There's a good-faith deposit."

Audrey stared down at the pile of bills. "You don't even know how much I charge to rent the place."

"Money's no problem. I just want that girl there."

"I'll do my best." Audrey picked up the bills and stuffed them into the low-cut top of her shirt inside her red, lace bra just barely visible. "No guarantees. I don't insist on my girls stripping. It's completely up to them."

"I'll be by tomorrow to sign papers."

Audrey leaned back, her brows forming a V over her nose, her lips quirking upward in a smile. "You're a pushy bastard, aren't you?"

"Only way to get what you want."

The woman chuckled. "And I'll bet you get what you want every time."

"That's my aim." He grinned and stuck out his hand. "I'll be by tomorrow. Tell my boys I'll see them at home." He nodded toward his sons, pushing their way through the crowd of men now standing around the horse and its bareback rider, catcalling and hooting with every move of the woman's luscious body. His boys had a thing for this Isabella. Her reluctance to perform as a stripper endeared her to Jonathon even more. She was modest and unassuming about her body. And damned sexy, even if she didn't think so. Even if she wasn't *the one*, she just might get his boys interested in finding a woman and settling down.

Audrey stood, tucking her hands into her back pockets. "Will do, Mr. O'Brien. Drive safely."

His duty done, Jonathon left the Ugly Stick Saloon and

headed back to the Rockin' O Ranch, more than determined to see his boys settled.

WHEN THE RAUCOUS cowboy song ended, Isabella had been more than ready to dismount her gallant machine and change into her uniform of cutoff jeans, tank top and cowboy boots. Normally, she wouldn't be caught dead struttin' around in a bikini and cheesy chaps. But when she saw the amount of money the cowboys were throwing on the floor at her feet, she couldn't just walk away. One more song. She could ride for one more song.

Though dancing half-naked in front of a bunch of drunken cowboys wasn't her thing, Isabella had to remind herself that it was all for a good cause. And they didn't seem to mind that she wasn't quite as busty as the other girls, or that she wasn't as graceful and sexy. One of Audrey's requirements of her *girls* was that they either sang or danced in order to get hired on as a waitress at the Ugly Stick Saloon. Since Isabella couldn't carry a tune in a bucket, she'd opted to dance. Not that she'd done much dancin' on the horse ranch. Dancing was like having sex, only in public. And Isabella didn't consider herself sexy.

As liquored up as these men were, anything with a vagina would be sexy to them.

Still, this was her first time performing by herself and she was anything but a performer. Give her a real horse and a decent pair of jeans and she'd show them what real riding was. The sexy outfit was just for show. She hoped it did the trick. Being a sex object had never been one of her goals in life and she wasn't so sure she had all the right equipment to qualify. Her body wasn't shaped like the other girls, and she didn't have the moves. Hell, she was more at home in a barn than in a bedroom. Her track record in relationships had proven that.

Because of her failed love life, she needed this job and the money she could earn through tips. She was saving to buy back Sundance before her ex sold the horse at auction. No amount of tips from waiting tables would add up fast enough to cover the cost of the thoroughbred horse. She needed a way to make big bucks quick. Perhaps this mechanical horse gig would be her ticket.

When the band played a sexy, swaying melody, Isabella motioned for Jackson to switch the horse into a slower, more sensuous action. More capable of holding on with only a light touch, Isabella closed her eyes and imagined herself in another place, a place where she could ride Sundance bareback across lush green fields of hay. The music filled her, dancing and swaying all around, her body moving to the gentle rhythm, her mind entering another dimension, one in which her body ignited and her core heated to molten levels. Wearing nothing but a bikini and chaps, she could imagine all kinds of sexy, naughty things she could do alone with herself or with a man…or men…who knew what it took to please her.

That's where her relationship with her ex-boyfriend, Daniel, had gone wrong. He'd been frustrated and finally insulted that he couldn't get her off. No amount of fore-play on his part brought her to orgasm. Sweet-talk or Daniel's hands sliding across her skin hadn't brought her to that elusive climax she craved, not that Daniel spent a whole lot of time pleasing her. When she didn't come within five minutes of trying, he blamed her and went on about the act of screwing her, calling her frigid and the ice queen.

Isabella's chest constricted. Maybe she was frigid. She'd never considered herself sexy, why should anyone else?

She should have ended their association before it had come to a boiling point. Then maybe Daniel wouldn't have been such a dick about Sundance, the horse she'd raised since he was a gangly colt, all legs and no coordination, her only true friend in this crazy, mixed-up world. He'd been a gift from her father.

Sundance had won his first three races, the long shot, coming out of nowhere, attracting the attention of the Circle C Ranch, who'd made an offer to purchase him.

Isabella had refused to sell, until that fateful day her parents were involved in a tragic automobile accident, killing her father and confining her mother to a hospital bed for several months before she gave up and died. Everything, including their home and property, went to paying off the medical bills and still, it wasn't enough. Isabella had been forced to sell Sundance to the Circle C Ranch. Fortunately, they'd offered her a job caring for him and the other thoroughbreds. That seemed like so long ago. Now she worked at the Ugly Stick Saloon and she hadn't seen Sundance in six months, although she'd followed his track statistics.

Isabella leaned over the mechanical horse's back, pretending to ride like the wind, trying to forget for the moment how much she missed her horse. Someone stuck a riding crop in her hand and she tapped it against her thigh. She'd never used one on Sundance.

A roar of approval rose from the crowd of men, prompting Isabella to open her eyes, reminding her of where she was.

She tapped the crop to her ass and more bills floated to the floor at the base of the imitation horse. *Hmmm. This could be lucrative.* All she had to do was pretend to like a little whip action and the men went wild. Her pussy tightened. Maybe it wasn't all pretending and she wasn't as frigid as Daniel thought.

She arched her back and ran one hand up her side to cup her breast, the other hand rose to lightly tap the crop against her other breast, drawing it across the tip and down the center of her cleavage. The leather against her skin sent heat radiating downward to where her cunt slid across the smooth back of the horse. *This could be addictive.*

"She's so hot, I'm gonna come!" One cowboy cried out, whipping his hat from his head to fan the front of his jeans.

"Keep it in your pants, George. I'm gonna marry that girl." Another cowboy dropped to his knees. "Marry me, Isabella."

Isabella laughed, pressing a hand to her chest, the crop clutched tightly in her fist. Maybe she was going too far with the sexy vamp thing. Maybe she was getting off a little more than she'd intended. Her eyes widened. Hell, she *was* getting off. By herself. Without a man...a miracle as far as her ex was concerned. Her ego took a leap.

"More! We want more!" The men surged forward, jockeying for position at the front of the line.

Jackson Gray Wolf stepped out front, crossing his arms. "Back off!"

"Come on, Jackson, you're blocking the view." A burly man in dusty jeans and a wife-beater shirt lumbered forward. "We wanna see her ride bareback."

Jackson held his ground. "Back up and I'll consider moving. Be a jerk and the show's over."

The men behind the big burly cowboy yelled at him, "Get back, George, we wanna watch."

"Move it, cowboy."

"Let her ride!" A bigger guy than wife-beater-shirt reached out and pulled the obnoxious one out of the way.

Isabella breathed a sigh. One of the O'Brien men. Gabe, she remembered from the time he'd asked her out, shortly after she'd arrived at the Ugly Stick. She'd considered going out with him, but it had been too soon after Daniel dumped her.

At least Gabe wasn't obnoxious like the wife-beater. Still, he looked as hot and bothered as the rest of them, his jeans tight around the groin area. Based on the swell, he had a real boner going there.

Another twinge of excitement nudged at her core. The rocking action of the horse, the feel of leather in her hands and the sight of a handsome aroused man, a gentleman cowboy to boot, all added up to turning her on. Too bad Daniel hadn't figured that out. Then she wouldn't be missing Sundance and wondering when she'd ever see him again. And that was the reason she'd stayed so long with Daniel. The horse. Not the man.

A toothless cowboy surged forward. Jackson cut him off before he reached Isabella.

What would she have done if Jackson hadn't been there to ward off unwanted attention and groping by the drunks in the saloon? Isabella longed for the wide-open spaces of a ranch where she could get away from the crowds.

What she wouldn't give to be doing what she loved the most, working with horses on a large horse ranch. Not that she didn't appreciate all that Audrey had done for her. If it hadn't been for Audrey and the Ugly Stick Saloon, she'd be on the street, flat broke with no way of earning enough money to keep her afloat, much less have any chance in hell of buying her horse from Daniel.

If only she could earn the money faster. She knew that if Daniel couldn't get Sundance to win the next two races, he'd have the horse up on the auction block. Isabella had been the only handler who could work with the horse. The only one who knew how Sundance operated.

The thoroughbred racehorse responded to light nudges, not heavy-handed whipping with a riding crop. Knowing Daniel, he'd gone right to using the crop to get the horse to move. Maybe even out of spite for Isabella's departure. And when Sundance wouldn't respond, Daniel would have blamed Isabella.

Yes, she should have gotten out of that poisonous relationship earlier. She would have, if not for Sundance. Instead, she'd stayed at the Circle C Ranch, working for Daniel and his mother, training and caring for the race-horses until Daniel had fired her as a girlfriend and horse trainer.

Now the closest she'd gotten to a horse was riding the mechanical horse at the Ugly Stick. Which hadn't been as bad as she'd thought it would be. For some strange reason, the rocking motion, the audience of aroused men and the leather crop combined had given her a bigger charge than she'd felt in a long time. Had she been a man, she'd leave the stage with a hard-on. As it was, she felt all warm and wet and ready for anything.

The music ended and Isabella sat for a moment, reining in her lusty thoughts.

Three tall, dark-haired cowboys slid past Jackson and held out their hands to her. Ah, yes, the handsome O'Briens.

Her belly tightened and a rush of heat pooled even lower. Strong, healthy cowboys always held a soft spot in her heart and a hot spot elsewhere. Especially these three. They'd all asked her out at one time. She'd been too freshly rejected by Daniel to even consider dating at the time. And they hadn't asked her again.

"Let me help you down." The oldest, Gabe O'Brien, held out his hands.

She brushed them aside. "I can get down on my own." Because she was in such a heightened sense of arousal, she couldn't risk letting a man touch her intimately. Not now. Besides, she didn't need a man to help her off a horse, real or mechanical. She slid her leg over the smooth fiberglass body of the horse and dropped to the ground, forgetting it was a little higher than the platform the mechanical horse was attached to.

Tanner, another of the O'Brien men caught her,

pulling her against his hard chest to steady her. "Are you okay?"

His breath stirred tendrils of hair near her ear, sending all kinds of shivery shards of electricity bouncing off her skin. "I'm fine." Again, she had to remind herself she didn't need a man in her life. The previous one had ruined her, making her think she didn't have a romantic or erotic bone in her body.

Then why, when Tanner's hands circled her waist, had her body ignited and her breath lodged in her throat?

She'd gone almost six months without a man and Daniel hadn't gotten her as excited during her year-long relationship as the O'Brien men had in less than a second.

Probably because she'd gone six months without any sex. One time with Tanner and she'd be bored and unable to reach that elusive orgasm she'd been longing for, going on a year and a half.

His hands moved lower, curving over her hips. "Would you care to dance?"

"He's got two left cowboy boots." Sean O'Brien stepped up to Isabella. "Dance with me. I, at least, can do a decent two-step."

Gabe shook his head. "Give the gal some room to breathe, guys." He held out his hand. "She's not interested."

Gabe's commanding voice captured Isabella's attention and without thinking, she put her hand in his.

He extricated her from his brother's arms and led her several steps away. "You make riding bareback an experience that bears watching." Lifting her hand, he turned it over and pressed a kiss to her palm. "Thank you." Then he dropped her hand. "Come on, Tanner, Sean. Leave her alone."

"But, she didn't say no to the dance," Sean argued, his smile turning full-force on Isabella. "Well?"

The younger O'Brien's grin was infectious and Isabella couldn't help returning his smile with a little shake of her head. "Sorry, I have to get back to work."

Tanner lifted his cowboy hat. "Thank you for a great show, ma'am."

With that, the three O'Brien men walked back to their table and sat.

Isabella's brows furrowed as she headed back to the dressing room where she could change into her cutoffs, tank top and cowboy boots, each of the O'Brien men on her mind. All of them as tall as church steeples, broad-shouldered and sun-kissed from working outside. Her dormant sex drive kicked up, reminding her that she was a young female with needs, not a dried-up old biddy. Following on the heels of that thought was the echo of Daniel's parting words. *A man wants to know he can make his woman as hot as she makes him. You bring nothing to that table, lady.*

For the past six months, Isabella had believed that. Bumping into the O'Briens made her think perhaps she wasn't as frigid as Daniel made her out to be. Too bad, she wasn't interested in testing that theory. God forbid Daniel might be right.

Her belly tightened and her pussy throbbed.

Or was she just frightened by the intensity of the heat roiling inside her body at the mere thought of going out with one of the O'Brien men?

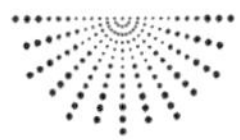

Gabe sat at the table, nursing his beer, watching for when Isabella emerged from the back room behind the bar. "Maybe Dad's got a point."

"What? Don't tell me you're buying into that *find one before all the good ones are gone* bullshit?" Tanner shook his head. "I'm not ready to go running after a woman just because Dad says we're getting old. Been there, done that, got the scars to prove it."

"You went after the wrong woman, Tanner. Don't paint them all with the same brush as Lucy." Sean patted his brother's back. "You can't let one woman turn you against all of them."

Tanner crossed his arms. "Who said I was?"

"Have you been out on a date since Lucy ditched you over a year ago?"

"Yes, plenty."

"How about a second date?" Sean persisted.

Tanner's lips thinned. "So, they weren't right for me. Why drag it out?"

"Think about it," Gabe said. "Jesse's getting married. He's the youngest."

"No, Molly's the youngest," Tanner interjected.

"Of the men, dumbass." Gabe focused on the door leading to the storeroom and backstage. "Isabella is single, isn't she? She's not hiding a husband somewhere, is she?"

"As far as I know she isn't married." Tanner's eyes narrowed. "Now, wait a minute. I saw her first."

"Like hell you did." Sean leaned forward. "Besides, you're not interested in running after women." He nodded toward a duded-up cowboy. "Maybe he's more your style."

Tanner rose, his fist clenched. "That's not what I said. And you're right. Isabella's different—nothin' like Lucy."

"Forget it. You two are too young for Isabella, anyway." Gabe set his beer on the table. "She's too much for both of you to handle. It will take a real man to win her over."

Tanner snorted. "Well that would rule you out. When were you ever in a lasting relationship?"

Gabe bristled. "I've been in relationships."

Sean's brows rose. "Yeah. The longest one lasting… what…all of two weeks before you started feeling hemmed in and dropped her like a hot branding iron?"

"I'd call that being allergic to commitment." Tanner's lips quirked upward in an almost smile.

Gabe wanted to punch both of his brothers for being way too close to the truth. "A man can change."

"Uh-huh. Right." Sean shook his head.

"We'll see." Anger spurred Gabe to action.

"Wait a minute." Tanner's hand shot out, grabbing Gabe's arm. "Where do you think you're going?"

Gabe stared at Tanner's hand. "Gonna see a man about a horse, and I don't need you to unzip my pants."

Tanner let go of Gabe's arm. "Reckon you can manage on your own."

"Your confidence overwhelms me." Gabe chuckled and strode toward the men's room. Halfway there, he shot a quick glance behind him.

Tanner's attention had returned to the dance floor.

Good.

Gabe veered toward the back of the bar where Isabella had disappeared, slipping past Greta Sue, the bouncer, when she wasn't looking. He had to get Isabella alone.

His father had been right. He hadn't been persistent in pursuing Isabella. Gabe figured it was about time to get serious and see where things went. What was the worst that could happen?

She could say no again.

Gabe refused to take no for an answer. He just needed to turn up the O'Brien charm.

In the hallway leading to the rear exit, he ducked his head into the storeroom. Empty. He followed the hallway to the back room that comprised the back of the stage and the costume room that held all the costumes for stripper night at the saloon.

Isabella stood with her back to him, struggling to untie the red bikini strap around her neck.

Gabe stood stock-still; his heart thundered and his breath labored.

The woman was beautiful, slender and athletic, legs

from her toes to her chin. Without trying, she had a natural grace in every movement. Her long, luxurious hair reached her waist, skimming across the top of her low-riding bikini bottoms.

Gabe wanted to bury his hands in her curls, and his cock in…

Isabella sighed, her hands falling to her sides, the knot at her neck remaining tangled.

Apparently she hadn't heard Gabe enter, the noise and music from the bar drowning out his footsteps.

He cleared his throat and entered the room. "Can I help you with that?"

She started and swung to face him, her hand holding the bikini bra against her breasts. "What are you doing back here?"

Gabe smiled. "Looking for you."

"Didn't you see the *Employees Only* sign?" She frowned, standing there in nothing but the red bikini and looking good enough to eat, one lick at a time.

"I chose to ignore it. I wanted to see you."

She snorted. "Well, you've gotten an eyeful, now leave." Isabella pointed toward the door.

Gabe leaned against the doorjamb. "You look like you could use a hand untying that."

"I can manage, thank you very much."

"No, really, let me help." He pushed away from the doorjamb and closed the distance between them. "I promise not to do anything…you don't want me to."

She snorted again, but didn't argue.

He moved around behind her and grasped the knot.

"You were great out there tonight," he said softly, while working the fabric loose.

"Thanks." She stood with her hands pressed to her bikini bra, her long, dark hair hanging down over one shoulder. "Felt strange riding a mechanical horse. I'm used to the real deal."

He couldn't help that his knuckles brushed against the smooth skin at the back of her neck or that the curve of her waist and the crease disappearing into the back of her bikini bottoms was wreaking all kinds of havoc, making his jeans so tight he could hardly stand it. "You ride much?" God, he'd like to ride her.

"Used to," she whispered. Her body trembled beneath his touch.

Gabe suspected it wasn't so much from his touch as it was from some emotion she was feeling. "Why don't you ride anymore?"

She shrugged, one hand rising to brush at something on her cheek.

His finger freed the knot and he turned her in his arms. "Are you crying?"

Her lips pulled into a tight line as a single tear trickled down her cheek. "No, of course not."

Gabe tipped her chin and studied her face, his head shaking. "Liar." His thumb caught the tear, brushing it away. "Why don't you ride anymore?"

"I was fired from my last job as a horse trainer."

"You?" He leaned back, frowning. "You're one of the hardest working women in this place."

"Didn't get along with the owner's son." She leaned her

forehead into his chest. "All I ever wanted to do was take care of the horses. Now, the closest I can get to a horse is the mechanical one in the other room. God, I miss the real ones."

Gabe tightened his fingers around her arms, dragging her against his chest. He smoothed a hand down her long, silky hair, fighting the desire to thread his fingers through the tresses. "I take it the boss's son was a jerk?"

She dipped her head in a single nod. "Yeah. The worst part is that I was fool enough to think he really loved me. But I never quite measured up." Isabella smiled up at him. "That's the past, though. It was nice of you to listen."

Her lips were rosy and full. Totally kissable.

"If you ever need someone to listen, I'm all ears." Before he could stop himself, he slid his thumb across her bottom lip and followed it with a gentle butterfly kiss.

Isabella slid her hands up around his neck, urging him closer.

With her permission granted, Gabe claimed her, his tongue sliding past her teeth to thrust inside her warm, wet mouth. He slipped his hands down her naked back, dragging the strings of the bikini top with them.

She leaned her naked breasts into his shirt, setting his body on fire.

Gabe dug his fingers beneath the elastic band of her bikini bottom and cupped her ass, lifting her until her legs wrapped around his waist. "Just tell me to stop and I will."

She crossed her ankles behind him and rubbed her crotch over the ridge beneath his fly.

Gabe moaned into her mouth, reaching one-handed between them to loosen the button at his waistband and unzip.

His cock sprang free, nudging against the fabric of her bikini.

She shifted, dragging the material to the side so that his penis nudged against her opening. "Ride me, cowboy," she whispered.

He reached into his back pocket and yanked out his wallet. "Will you do the honors?" He shook it open.

Isabella located the foil packet he had tucked in with his money. He couldn't believe he was here, holding her so close, about to make love to her in the back of the bar with a crowd of people on the other side of the curtain.

"I can't believe I'm doing this. I must be insane. Something about riding that mechanical horse made me…"

He pressed a kiss to her lips. "Hot?"

"Wickedly horny." She ripped the packet open and tossed the foil over her shoulder, her fingers clutching the rubber.

Gabe shoved his wallet into his back pocket and held Isabella far enough away from him so that she could roll the rubber down over his dick, her fingers lingering to fondle his balls.

Blood pumping, his cock throbbing, Gabe could barely wait to thrust inside her, to feel her warm, slick channel contract around him.

"Just so you know, I didn't come back here for a quick fuck."

"I know." Her body quivered, gooseflesh rising on her arms. "But that's what I want. Are you afraid someone will catch us?"

"Hell yes."

"Me too. And it's making me hotter." She kissed him

hard. "Quick, before someone does."

Her words only made his cock swell more, the pressure so much, he feared he'd explode before he consummated their little tryst. "But what about you? This will be too fast. I want you to come too."

Ignoring his concern, she adjusted her thong, slipping it even further to the side, and lowered herself until her pussy kissed the head of his penis. "Hurry," she entreated, her arms wrapping around his neck.

The urgency in her voice reverberated through his body and he thrust up inside her.

She clamped her legs around his waist, her heels digging into his buttocks. Isabella threw back her head and rode him, nails digging into his shoulders.

Every unusual noise made Gabe jump and thrust deeper, his nerves on edge, his body burning from the intimate connection and the danger. The naughtiness of their deed struck him, rocketing him over the edge, his orgasm shaking him to his very core. Thrusting one last time, he held her down on him, his cock as deep as he could get, throbbing, spilling his seed into the protective contraceptive.

When he could breathe again, he dragged in a deep steadying breath. "Now, let me return the favor."

She ran her fingers through his hair, her legs tightening one more time before she unlocked her ankles from around his waist. "We don't have time."

He shook his head, reason pulling back on the reins of his lust. "But I want to get you there." He wanted her to be as aroused and ready as he was. "I want to pleasure you." He backed her against a vanity table, setting her bottom on the edge and withdrawing from her slick warmth. "Let me make you as hot as you make me." Gabe found her center, swirling his fingers around the juicy entrance. God, she was wet. He slipped one finger inside and dragged her juices upward, partying her folds to find the slender nubbin nestled between. He touched her there, flicking her clit, then he dropped to his knees, his mouth replacing his fingers. He sucked on her clit, his tongue tapped and teased, licking and flicking. "Don't you want this?" he whispered, blowing a warm stream of air across her damp pussy. "Can you feel it? Let me take you to the edge and make you come."

Her body stiffened.

He knew she'd withdrawn before he ever looked up into her eyes.

Her breath caught and held and she pressed her hands against his shoulders. "No. I can't." She gulped and looked away. "We shouldn't." Isabella shoved against him and dropped to her feet. "I don't know what came over me. I should get back to work. I'm on duty. This shouldn't be happening."

"I thought you liked it." Gabe rose, reflecting back through all he'd said, searching for whatever it was that had hit her Off switch. "Did I say something wrong?"

"No, no." She shook her head, ducking around him, searching the hooks on the wall for her cutoffs and tank top. "It's me. You really shouldn't be back here. Employees only, like I said. If Greta Sue finds you…" She pulled the tank top over her naked breasts and the denim shorts up over the bikini bottom. When she faced him, she frowned. "Just go."

Mentally scratching his head, Gabe removed the condom, zipped his fly, left the backstage area and returned to the bar. What had he said or done to make Isabella do a complete about-face? He thought they'd connected…not just got it on.

He returned to the table and sat between his brothers, confused, frustrated and once again uncomfortable in his jeans.

"Where have you been?" Tanner asked him.

"Bathroom, like I said. Too much beer," he muttered, his mood turning sour the more he sat there.

"Something making you sick? You look a little pale. Too many fried jalapeños?" Sean chuckled. "I don't see how you can stand to eat those."

Gabe didn't contradict his younger brother. He hadn't had a single one of the fried jalapeños Tanner had ordered. If anything, his gut hurt from the punch he'd received when Isabella had gone cold on him after he'd made love to her. And damn it, he hadn't done what he'd gone back there to do in the first place. He hadn't asked her out on a date. *Well, hell.* She probably thought he was a class-A jerk.

He'd be in the Ugly Stick Saloon every night that week if that was what it took to get Isabella to agree to go out with him. She felt right in his arms. Isabella Severs could be *the one* and Gabe meant to find out. Once he set his mind to something, he pursued it until it was his. And Gabe O'Brien had set his mind on Isabella.

Isabella hefted the heavy plastic tub filled with empty

mugs and trays onto the bar. She was ready to get out of the saloon and home to her own apartment where she could finally sit back and go over everything that had happened that night, in particular, what had happened between her and Gabe O'Brien. Holy crap, she'd made love to him in the back of the saloon when she was supposed to be working. So much for swearing off men.

"That's all the mugs and trash." Isabella wiped her hands against her cutoffs. "Need help washing up?"

Libby, the bartender, smiled, her hands in sudsy water up to her elbows. "No, I'm just about done. Why don't you head home?"

"I think I will. I'm exhausted and my feet are killing me." *And my pussy is raw and throbbing, ready for another go at the oldest O'Brien.*

"Isabella, you got a moment?" Audrey's voice floated out of the tiny storage room she'd converted into an office a month ago.

Isabella suppressed a groan, pushed her lusty thoughts aside and stepped into Audrey's office, collapsing into the beat-up, cracked leather chair on the opposite side of an equally worn desk. "What's up?"

Audrey tapped her pencil to a paper in front of her, biting down on the corner of her bottom lip. "I have a problem I think you can help me with, if you're willing." She glanced up, her tired eyes wide and hopeful.

"Shoot." Audrey had done so much for her, offering her a job and a room until she could get on her feet and afford her own apartment.

"Tonight I got a request for a bachelor's party for next week. I've been wanting to have the wood floors in this place stripped and waxed, but can never quite find enough spare cash to make it happen."

Isabella shrugged. "What's that got to do with me?"

"The man who asked to throw the party is willing to pay just about anything since it's such short notice and I think we can make enough off this one party to do the floors with some cash to spare. He even put down a thousand dollar deposit."

"Wow." Isabella leaned forward, ready to stand. "I think you should go for it."

"I can't." Audrey cringed. "He had one condition."

Isabella sank back into her seat. Audrey almost never beat around the bush. "What condition?"

"He wants *you* to be the stripper at the party."

Isabella popped out of her chair. "No."

Audrey smiled. "I told him you wouldn't, but that I would ask anyway."

"I'm not a dancer and I'd just look like a fool taking off my clothes. Besides, men don't think I'm sexy."

"Honey, did you see the reactions of the crowd tonight when you were riding the mechanical horse?" Audrey grinned. "You were all sex and sass. Every one of those men wanted you."

"They were drunk."

"Isabella, you've got all the right equipment, they wouldn't be disappointed with that."

"Even if I had the right look, I'm not a dancer. I'm a cowgirl who's used to taking care of horses, not men." Isabella strode to the door, hoping to end the conversation.

Audrey called out after her, "He'll pay you five

hundred dollars a dance."

Isabella stopped, her hands braced on the doorframe. Five hundred dollars a dance would go a long way toward earning the money she needed to buy Sundance.

"You could earn a lot of money in one night," Audrey added, dangling the carrot.

Isabella shouldn't even consider stripping to earn the money to buy Sundance. Her body wasn't a sexual treat like Lacey's. Her breasts were too small and her hips too slim. She didn't have a curvy ass like Kendall. Then why *was* she considering it? A trickle of excitement mixed with trepidation shivered across her skin. "Where will the bachelor party be?" Isabella turned toward her boss. "Not that I've agreed yet."

Audrey grinned. "Here. And you'd have access to all the costumes and equipment if you decide to do the mechanical horse again."

Still unwilling to commit, Isabella's eyes narrowed. "Would I have to take off *all* my clothes?"

Audrey shook her head. "Only as much as you feel comfortable with. The bikini and chaps tonight had the crowd more than appreciative."

A bikini was doable without going all naked. The emotional side of Isabella's brains was telling her to say no. "What if the men get too…touchy?" And discover she wasn't so sexy, or that she didn't have big boobs.

"I can have Greta Sue or one of the Gray Wolf brothers stick around to make sure nothing happens that you don't want to happen."

With all her concerns addressed, Isabella couldn't resist the temptation of the money. The deal was too good to pass up. Owning Sundance suddenly looked more achievable. "Five hundred dollars a dance?" Isabella's internal calculator started adding. "Is there a limit to the number of dances?"

"He said up to three dances. You have the opportunity to make fifteen hundred in one night. And that doesn't include any tips the men might throw your way. Where else can you make that kind of money?"

Nowhere. She really didn't have a choice if she wanted to buy Sundance anytime soon. With a deep breath, she dove in. "I'll do it."

Audrey smiled. "Thank God. This will mean a lot of money for you and the Ugly Stick. I can probably even have the exterior of the building painted with the money we'll make."

Isabella held up a finger. "One thing."

Audrey's grin slipped. "What?"

"Whose bachelor party is it?"

"Jesse O'Brien. His father, owner of the Rockin' O Ranch, is footing the bill. With over ten thousand acres and a herd the size of my hometown, I think he can afford it."

Isabella sucked in a sharp breath, her heart plummeting to the bottom of her belly. "The O'Briens?"

"That's right." Audrey glanced down at her ledger. "You know them?"

"Only from when they come into the saloon," she lied. She knew more about Gabe after tonight than she'd known the whole time he'd been frequenting the Ugly Stick. But Audrey didn't have to know what they'd done backstage.

"They're nice men, and all of them handsome." Audrey tapped her pencil to her bottom lip and glanced up. "If I wasn't happy with Jackson, I'd be looking for some fun with any one of the O'Brien boys—hell, maybe all of them —including their father. He's a firecracker and still good-looking. Must be closing in on sixty by now."

Audrey's words faded to the recesses of Isabella's mind as she gathered her purse and truck keys. Too wound up to go home to bed, she wandered back into the bar.

Libby had finished cleaning and left while Isabella and Audrey had been discussing business. With nothing but the exit lights glowing over the front door and a couple soft lights shining down over the stage and the bar, the saloon was eerily quiet. The mechanical horse stood to the side of the stage—the beast that had started every-thing. If not for it, Isabella would still be scrambling for a way to earn money fast. Now she had the opportunity she needed. Owning Sundance wasn't just a dream anymore.

Pushing aside her misgivings and self-doubts, she allowed a surge of joy to fill her chest. She wrapped her arms around her middle and squealed like a young girl.

"Anyone still in here?" Audrey switched the light on over the dance floor. "Oh, Isabella, it's you. Anything wrong?"

"Nothing. I was just thinking."

"About the offer?"

Isabella nodded. "I'll need to practice more to get ready."

"They won't care how you dance. As long as there's lots of skin, they'll be happy." Audrey's lips twisted. "Trust me. I know."

"With as much as they're willing to spend, I want them to get their money's worth." Isabella chewed on her bottom lip. "You think I'll do okay?"

"Honey, the way you rode that mechanical horse had them all panting like dogs. You'll do fine. But if you'd like some extra time to practice, you can use the saloon when it's closed. Hold on just a minute." Audrey ducked into her office and was back in seconds. She tossed a shiny metal object toward Isabella. "Now you have a key. Just lock up afterward."

Isabella's chest couldn't get any tighter. To have a boss who gave you a key to her saloon was a level of trust she'd never had. "Thanks, Audrey. You won't regret it. I'll be careful to lock up."

Audrey laid a hand on her arm. "I know you will. Good night, honey. Don't stay too late. I need you for tomorrow night. It's Girls' Night Out and we have male strippers coming. The place will be packed."

"Don't worry. I'll be here."

Audrey left the light on over the dance floor and exited through the back entrance.

Isabella was alone, the silence soothing, the empty dance floor her stage with no one to watch or laugh at her. She dug into her purse for some dollar bills and fed the juke box, selecting songs she thought might work for her three dances.

When the first one came on, she closed her eyes and swayed to the music, letting it fill her senses and take her away to a quiet place where she could loosen up and forget she trained horses. She was a woman with sexual needs and desires.

The fact that the O'Briens had asked for her specifically reverberated through her thoughts. All three of the young men had attempted to make a pass at her that night and many nights before that. But for the first time in a long time, she'd allowed herself to feel something besides terror. Alone on the dance floor, she gave in, letting that feeling blossom.

Even now, her body trembled, her belly tightening, her pussy clenching, a rush of juices warming her channel, still tender from Gabe's lovemaking.

Isabella chalked it up to desperation. Making love to even one of them didn't mean she would have an orgasm. She hadn't even given Gabe a chance to get her there. Too afraid of failing, she'd shut him down and run.

The outcome would be the same as when she'd been with Daniel. Nothing she'd tried had given her satisfaction. She'd tossed her vibrator when even it didn't leave her satisfied.

What did she care whether or not she could achieve the big 'O'? The party was a gig she couldn't afford to turn down. She wouldn't tempt herself into testing the waters with one of the O'Briens. She didn't want to experiment with her female ability with them anyway. How embarrassing if she couldn't get there or had to fake it. She was a terrible faker. It had been another reason Daniel had broken it off with her. No. Faking wasn't an option.

Face it. She was a horse girl, not a lover. She'd do the three dances, collect her money and go back to doing what came natural, taking care of horses and taking care of Sundance. In the meantime, she'd better come up with some moves to give them their money's worth.

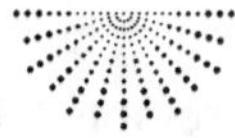

CHAPTER THREE

Gabe leaned against the tailgate of his truck parked at the back of the Ugly Stick Saloon, waiting for Isabella to get off work. He'd gone home when the others had called it a night. But as soon as they dropped down out of the truck, he made up the excuse of forgetting his wallet at the bar and having to go back to find it. His brothers had offered to help him, but he'd refused, saying it was probably under the table they'd sat at.

His wallet had been in his back pocket the entire time. He just wanted a shot at asking Isabella out before his brothers could get to her.

At two forty-five in the morning, Audrey emerged from the back door. She crossed to her bright red pickup truck, a smile curling her lips, her head tipping upward toward a star-studded sky.

To keep from startling her, Gabe called out, "Nice evening, isn't it?"

Audrey jumped, her eyes widening. "Gabe? Is that you?"

"Yes, ma'am." He removed his hat and let the moon shine down on his head, illuminating his face for her to identify.

"Please." She shook her head. "Don't call me ma'am. I'm not any older than you are."

"Yes, ma'am." He grinned.

"Whatcha hangin' around here for? The saloon closed forty-five minutes ago."

"I know. I was hoping to catch Isabella."

"She's inside, working on a project. I can let you in." She held up her keys.

"Thanks, I'd appreciate that."

"Good. I don't like leaving her here all by herself." Audrey led the way to the back door and inserted the key into the lock, then paused when headlights shone around the corner of the building.

A truck pulled into the rear parking area.

Audrey's brows pulled into a frown. "Expectin' company?"

"No, ma'am." The truck turned and parked. When two men dropped down out of it, Gabe sighed. "Looks like my brothers found me."

Her lips quirking, Audrey looked past him to Sean and Tanner. "I didn't realize you were lost."

"Wish they'd *get* lost." Gabe tapped his hat against his leg. "I wanted to get Isabella alone and ask her out."

"Is that right?" Audrey's brows rose. "Want me to stall them?"

"Yes, ma'am. I'd be mighty appreciative."

"You got it, cowboy. But I'll eventually have to let them in." She opened the door and hurried him inside. "Make it quick."

Gabe hustled through the backstage area, following the lights and music to the main room with the bar and dance floor. The scent of pine cleaner filled the air and most of the chairs had been stacked upside down on the tabletops.

At first he didn't see her. But then the repetitive sound of metal on metal reached his ears and his attention swung to the far side of the stage where the Gray Wolf brothers had moved the mechanical horse.

Isabella, in her cutoffs, boots and tank top swayed with the rhythm of the music and the rocking motion of the horse. With her eyes squeezed shut and her head tipped backward, her long tresses flowed down her back, brushing across the top of her buttocks.

Gabe's heart squeezed hard behind his rib cage. He'd never seen such beauty in motion before. He could only imagine how she'd look riding bareback on a real horse. Drawn like a bee to honey, he crossed the floor, his boots barely making a whisper on the hardwood. The music volume, set for a full dancehall, drowned out any other noises.

When he stood in front of the woman, he stopped, reluctant to pull her out of her trance, but aware of the short amount of time he had to ask her out.

Eyes still closed, Isabella smiled, the glow on her face ethereal, stunning and completely relaxed.

Gabe hated to interrupt whatever thought was giving her so much pleasure, at the same time a twinge of jealousy hit him in the gut. "What's making you smile, pretty Isabella?"

Isabella's eyes popped open, she lost her balance and pitched forward, toppling from the mechanical horse.

Gabe dove for her and caught her in his arms to steady her.

She rested her hands on his chest, her breathing coming in short gasps. "Damn, you scared the fool out of me."

Gabe chuckled. "Sorry. I didn't mean to. I just wanted to finish our conversation from earlier."

"You could have warned me." The smile that had graced her face had disappeared. She glanced up, her eyes narrowing as she peered up into his face. "Do you always lurk around empty saloons in the earliest part of the morning?" Her hands still lay flat against his chest and she'd made no move to disengage from his embrace.

His groin tightened at the feel of her hips moving against his. Heat flowed through his body, his fingers spreading across her lower back. "Not normally. But it was the only time I could get you alone."

"What is it you want?" she asked, her voice soft and breathy.

"To ask you out."

She tipped her head to the side. "Why couldn't you ask me when you were here earlier?"

"I got a little…distracted, and then you were in a hurry to get back to work. With my brothers there…" He shook his head. "I wanted to catch you alone."

She nodded. "It's a shame. I would have told you the same thing I'm going to tell you now, and you could have saved the trouble of coming back. I'm not interested." She attempted to push away.

Gabe's gut clenched. "What about what happened backstage?"

"It was a one-time thing." She pressed against his chest. "Please, let me go."

His fingers tightened around her hips. "Not until you tell me what I did wrong."

"You didn't do anything wrong. It was me."

"What?" He gripped her chin and urged her to look up at him. "What do you mean, it was you?"

"Look, I enjoyed having sex with you."

"But it was all one-sided. I didn't get a chance to make you happy."

She pushed his hands away. "What is it with men who think they have to make a woman orgasm? What happened to a man getting off and calling it done?"

"You ran because you didn't want an orgasm?"

She hung her head. "Can't."

"What do you mean 'can't'?" He turned her in his arms. "You're not making any sense."

"I can't have an orgasm, dammit!" Her chin lifted and she stared at him through watery eyes. "Are you happy now? You can't turn me on, because I don't have an On switch."

Gabe wanted to laugh, but the tears in her eyes made him hold back. "How do you know you can't have an orgasm?"

"Because I've tried."

His brows furrowed. "With your ex-boyfriend? Is he the reason you don't think you have it in you?" *That bastard.* Gabe wanted to take the guy out for causing Isabella to believe she was defective.

"This is silly. We don't even know each other that well and I'm spilling my guts. Just leave it, will you?"

"Give me a chance. Let me show you that it's not you."

"No. I'm done trying. I can't handle any more humiliation." She grabbed his shirt front and wadded her fist in it. "And don't you dare tell a soul what I just said. Not even your brothers. I'm enough of a failure without everyone else reminding me." She scrubbed her other hand over her eyes, wiping away any traces of tears.

Gabe's hand closed over her fist. "You're not a failure, Isabella. Let me prove it. Just one date."

"No."

At that moment, Tanner and Sean strode into the barroom.

"Lost your wallet, my ass," Tanner grumbled, striding forward.

"Only gonna be gone a minute…huh!" Sean closed in on Gabe and Isabella.

His brothers stood with their arms crossed.

"I found my wallet," Gabe offered, refusing to let go of Isabella.

"In your back pocket?" Tanner nodded toward Gabe's backside.

"No…really…"

Sean waved a hand, dismissing Gabe's excuse. "We figured you'd come back to talk to Isabella and we couldn't let you get away with it."

"Someone want to tell me what's going on?" Isabella

pushed away from him and shoved the hair out of her face.

Gabe was forced to let go, when he wanted to crush her in a bear hug and hold her until the hurt in her eyes went away. "Like I said, I wanted to ask you out."

"And so did we." Tanner poked a thumb toward Sean.

"I got here first." Gabe frowned at his brothers.

"It doesn't matter." Sean stepped forward. "Let the lady decide for herself." His frown switched into a smile. "What do you say, Isabella? Which one of us would you like to go out with?"

Isabella rolled her eyes. "Really? That's what this is all about?" She shook her head and turned toward the stage, collecting her purse and keys, her hands shaking. "Sorry, fellas. Like I told Gabe, I'm not interested." With that, she ducked past them, heading for the exit, shutting off the lights as she went.

If Gabe hadn't moved out of her way, he was sure she would have walked right over him without batting an eyelid.

He and his brothers followed.

Once outside, Isabella locked the back door, tested the lock and gave them all a pointed look. "Why are you still here?"

Gabe frowned. "I had hoped you'd change your mind."

"Not likely." She waved her hands at them. "Shoo! All of you. I'm not interested in going out with any of you, so don't bother." She left them standing there and climbed into a battered truck, pulling out of the parking lot, the tires kicking up gravel and dust.

Gabe glared at his brothers. "See what you did?"

"What *we* did?" Tanner's fists clenched. "You weren't making much headway by the looks of things."

"I was just getting started." Gabe's gaze followed Isabella's retreat.

"By the look of it…" Sean stood staring at the taillights disappearing down the gravel road leading to the highway, "we all struck out."

Tanner nodded. "Yeah, guess we did."

"Well, damn." Sean shoved a hand through his hair. "Wonder what it's gonna take to get her to say yes?"

"A lot more than we have to offer, that's what." Tanner gave Gabe a narrow-eyed glare. "No more tricks, brother."

"I don't see anything wrong with my wanting to ask Isabella out. And if you two hadn't come along, she eventually would have said yes."

"Yeah, right." Sean grinned. "Keep tellin' yourself that. You might believe it one day."

"I know exactly what she needs," Gabe muttered half to himself.

"Uh-huh. Right." Tanner shook his head. "Our brother is delusional. The woman isn't interested."

Gabe brushed past his brothers and climbed into his truck. They'd see. He'd get Isabella to go out with him if it was the last thing he did. And he'd prove to her that she wasn't defective, that she could enjoy sex, despite her ex-boyfriend's claim.

DESPITE HER VOW TO stay clear of the O'Briens except for her bachelor party commitment, Isabella ran into Tanner at the Sweet Temptations Diner two days later.

"Please, have lunch with me." He held the door open for her, sun glinting off his green eyes, his sensuous lips almost breaking a smile.

Isabella sighed. "Okay, but it's not a date."

"Fair enough." He nodded. "Just lunch between two friends."

The waitress showed them to a table in the corner and Tanner held her chair for her. His mamma had taught him well how to behave around a woman.

How nice. Daniel never held her chair. For that matter, he'd rarely taken her out to dinner or lunch or even for a friggin' cup of coffee.

Sitting across the table from the broad-shouldered Tanner, Isabella folded her hands in her lap, crossing her legs at the ankles, suddenly feeling more feminine than she had in a long time. More feminine than she had felt wearing the red bikini at the saloon the other night. And all that femininity made her body warm and excited.

She forced herself to relax and smile when she'd rather strip his shirt off and see what all that muscle looked like beneath the fabric. Squashing the image, she asked, "Why are you in town today? I'd think you'd be out working with the horses or cattle."

He shifted in the chair, his tanned complexion taking on a ruddy tinge. "I had some...errands to run." Tanner lifted his menu and studied it until the redness subsided.

"Did you come to town just to have lunch with me?"

His color deepened again and he sighed. "Was it that obvious?"

Isabella chuckled. "No, but I'm touched. I'm sure you

have more important things to do than lurk around town, waiting for me to get out of bed in time for lunch."

His brows dipped. "I wasn't lurking. And how else was I going to get time alone with you?"

Cute. A big, tough cowboy embarrassed?

Isabella's heart warmed. Not only was the man extremely drool-worthy, but a girl could fall for a guy like Tanner's soft-spoken, quiet ways. He didn't seem a bit egotistical or full of his own importance. He was just a good man. One worth loving, just like his brothers.

They spent lunch discussing the best way to train horses and hauling hay in the summer. When the waitress brought the bill, Isabella insisted on paying her half. "It's not a date, remember?"

Tanner's brows furrowed in a ready frown, giving him the appearance of a grouchy bear, making Isabella want to kiss away the lines on his forehead. Before she could act on her impulse, she slapped some money on the table and shoved out her hand. "Thanks for keeping me company, *friend.*"

When he grasped her hand, electric shocks skittered up her arm, spreading throughout her body.

"Would you consider going out with me?" he asked.

Friend didn't quite encompass the naughty thoughts Isabella had at that moment. She began to regret her self-imposed prohibition on the opposite sex. "I don't think it's a good idea. But thanks for asking." She hustled out of the diner and headed for the little lingerie shop, Naughty Nothings, a couple doors down, ducking in before Tanner could follow.

"Hi, Isabella, can I help you?" Molly O'Brien touched her arm.

Isabella jerked upright, her cheeks burning. "I…uh… need…" She glanced around the store, realization sinking in that she was in a sexy shop, talking with the sister of the guys she'd been having crazy sexual fantasies about. "I'm just looking."

Molly glanced past Isabella. "Oh, there's Tanner, and look, there's Gabe and Sean." She waved through the window. "Yoo-hoo!"

Isabella ducked past Molly and hurried to the back of the store, glancing at the door through her peripheral vision.

All three men ducked into the tiny shop, filling it with their wide shoulders and utter maleness.

"About time you came in to check out my day job." Molly hugged each of her brothers and then waved her hands toward the interior. "What do you think about my store?"

"Nice," Sean said, his gaze going for Isabella. "Hi, Isabella."

"Yeah, some pretty things in here." Gabe fingered a pair of sheer panties.

Isabella waved from across the small room, heat suffusing every part of her body. Then she turned away and pretended to inspect the merchandise in front of her until she realized they were sexy teddies lined with faux fur, complete with fuzzy handcuffs to match.

"You boys better get out of here. You're blocking the doorway." Molly shooed them through the door.

Isabella let out the breath she'd been holding and took

a really good look at the things she'd been pretending to study. "Holy crap, do women really wear this kinda stuff?"

"Oh, yes. I sell a lot of the red teddy and cuffs. And you wouldn't believe who buys them." Molly winked at Isabella. "I hear you're the entertainment at my brother's bachelor party. Were you looking for anything in particular for the event?"

"I…" Isabella stared around the shop, completely overwhelmed by all the pretty, sexy, naughty items. Her shoulders sagged. "I'm just a cowgirl. I wouldn't know where to begin."

Molly's eyes lit and she slipped an arm around Isabella's waist. "Well, honey, let me help."

Out of her depth, Isabella let Molly take the lead. An hour later, she walked out of the store with a red-sequined bikini top and a matching vest and thong.

The thong had Isabella the most worried. How in hell was she going to strip to a thong in front of all those men? If they had any doubts walking into the saloon that she didn't have the ass to jiggle, by the time they left, they'd be certain.

As she exited the store, she almost ran into Sean, leaning against the wall.

"Need some help?" He reached for the bag she carried.

Isabella jerked it back. "No. I don't need help. What are you doing here?"

"Thought I'd walk you home."

"What is it about you O'Brien men that you can't take no for an answer?"

He grinned. "We're stubborn." He leaned over her arm,

peering into the bag. "Whatdya buy? Silk panties, edible underwear, stockings and garters?"

Despite his prying, he was too cute to be mad at. She wrinkled her brows. "Do I look like the stockings and garters kinda girl?" She glanced down at her jeans and cowboy boots.

Sean's eyes lit. "Absolutely. I believe every woman has an inner vixen, begging to get out."

"Only a man would say that."

He shook his head. "Actually, I got that off my sister, Molly." He cringed. "Although hearing her say it gave me the willies. She's my baby sister, for God's sakes."

Isabella laughed out loud and let him draw her free hand through his arm. "I didn't say you could walk me home."

"Ah, but you didn't say I couldn't." He strode forward, smiling and confident.

Isabella could stand there and argue or go along with him. Either way, she needed to get home and start getting ready for work. If it meant walking with a handsome man on the sidewalk, so be it. Having other women give her envious stares was a novelty Isabella discovered that she enjoyed. Perhaps there was something to that inner vixen.

"How is it to be a middle child in the O'Brien family?" Isabella asked.

His eyes narrowed for a moment. "It can be challenging and yet easy. I don't have the burden of being oldest and having to set the example for my other siblings, but I never take for granted the family name." He shrugged. "I guess I'm more carefree than my brothers. Not that I don't work just as hard."

"I don't doubt that in the least." Isabella squeezed his muscle, enjoying how thick and hard it was, her thoughts going to the bulge behind his fly, her gut tightening. She wondered if he was thick and hard all over. His youth and enthusiasm would make him a lot of fun in bed. That thought immediately led to the other brothers. Were they as thick and hard all over? Would they satisfy her in bed?

She let go of his arm and nodded toward her apartment building. "I can take it from here."

"Better yet, I'll race you there."

"Your legs are longer."

"You can have a head start." His green eyes twinkled. "Ready? Go!"

Caught up in Sean's playfulness and eager to be away from temptation, Isabella tore out, running for her apartment.

Halfway down the block, Sean passed her and stopped on the steps.

When Isabella slowed to a halt, Sean swung her up in his arms, laughing.

"That's what I like about you, Isabella," he said as he set her back on her feet, his arm retaining its hold around her waist.

Breathless, Isabella smiled up at him. "What's that?"

"That you're fearless. You aren't afraid of anything."

Her smile faded. "I have to go."

Sean frowned. "So soon? Do you need me to carry your bag upstairs for you?" He pulled her close, his fly rubbing against hers, reminding her of how much he turned her on, as well as of the fact that she was anything but fearless about one thing. And that one thing had her petrified.

"I really need to go." She ducked beneath his arms and took the steps two at a time, pushing through the door to her apartment building.

God, she was a fool to think she could play with fire. Getting involved with the O'Brien men would only burn her.

CHAPTER FOUR

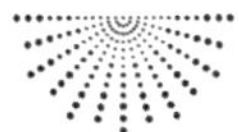

*I*sabella ducked into the storeroom the following Friday night at fifteen minutes to midnight, escaping the noise, yelling and sloshed drinks. Tonight, after the bar closed early at the unheard-of hour of midnight, she'd perform for the bachelor party. Her costume of the sequined red bikini top with a matching thong bottom, the sequined vest and glossy, black faux-leather chaps hung in the room behind the stage.

The Gray Wolf brothers stood ready to move the mechanical horse onto the stage once the band cleared out. All the music they needed would be provided by the open juke box, rigged to play for free after the regulars left.

For Isabella, the week had flown by. Everywhere she'd turned, an O'Brien had been there, wooing her, bringing her flowers, leaving chocolates and notes at her doorstep. What would it take to get rid of them?

She couldn't start something with any one of the

brothers without turning the others down. And they were all so darned charming and good-looking, she couldn't decide which she liked most.

Not that it mattered. Isabella Severs wasn't in the market for a man. No matter how sexy he was or how aroused she became when any one of the O'Brien men were around. She'd spent too many sleepless nights already fantasizing about Gabe. Problem was that she fantasized over Tanner and Sean, as well. How wrong was that? Couldn't she dream about one man alone? Sometimes she made love with just one at a time, but ultimately, all three ended up in her bed in her dreams, pleasuring her, wooing her with their hands, their tongues and other parts of their anatomy. And every time, she startled awake, tears in her eyes when the apparitions shook their heads, disappointed that she couldn't come, no matter how hard they tried.

Isabella couldn't bear to open herself up to failure. She'd even considered going to a doctor to have him check her over. Maybe her orgasm muscle was defective. The humiliation of discussing her sex life with the local doctor paled in comparison to failure to attain the female equivalent of *getting off* in the presence of the handsome cowboys.

No matter how horny she was getting, or how handsome the men were, she couldn't...no, she *wouldn't* put herself through that mortification again.

However, the flowers, notes and sweets had been so nice. And all three of the men had been complete gentlemen, courting her the old-fashioned way.

Maybe that was another one of her problems. Maybe

she needed less gentlemanly behavior. That way if she did happen to sleep with one of them again, he wouldn't notice if she didn't orgasm. He'd get in, get out, satisfying his own urges, never minding that he hadn't satisfied hers. She could deal with that better than being singled out for inability to perform.

"Five minutes to showtime," Greta Sue's voice boomed through the back of the saloon.

Isabella's breathing grew more labored, and her heart raced, pain ripping through her chest each time she inhaled. Good lord, was she having a heart attack?

She pressed a hand to her ribs and doubled over.

A gentle hand smoothed her hair back from her face. "Are you all right?"

Isabella glanced up into Audrey's concerned face. "I can't seem to get enough air."

Audrey smiled and handed her a paper lunch bag. "Breathe into this."

Her brow furrowing, Isabella shook her head and gasped. "I told you, I can't breathe."

"Try." Audrey shoved the bag over Isabella's mouth. "In with the good air, out with the bad," she chanted, repeating the phrase several times.

Audrey's persistence and softly spoken words had a gradual effect on Isabella and soon her breathing returned to normal, the pain in her chest receding. Finally, she straightened. "Thank God. I thought I was going to die."

"That's how I felt the first time I stripped."

"Does it get any easier?"

"Sometimes." Audrey shrugged. "It depends on the crowd."

"And the crowd out there now?"

"From what Jonathon O'Brian told me, they only invited four close friends of the groom. Those plus the groom and his three brothers makes eight. Nine, if you count Jonathon. But he doesn't plan on staying. He's afraid he'll cramp the boys' style." Audrey grinned. "That particular O'Brien is a gentleman."

Isabella sighed. "All of them are."

Audrey's brows rose. "Accept any of their invitations yet?"

"How can I choose? They're all equally handsome and charming."

"Don't forget sexy."

"Did I hear my name?" Jackson Gray Wolf ducked his head into the storeroom and smiled. "The horse is in place."

"Perfect timing." Audrey wrapped an arm around his neck and kissed the big Kiowa cowboy, her red-booted foot sliding up his calf, her body melting against his, her pussy riding his thick thigh.

Jackson's hand slipped into the waistband of Audrey's cutoffs, cupping her bottom.

Isabella squirmed, her nipples tightening at the blatant sexuality the couple exuded. A minute passed and Isabella's core throbbed. Finally, she cleared her throat. "I should go get ready." Problem was…they were blocking the exit.

Audrey pulled back, her lips swollen, her face flushed. "What? Oh, yeah. Right." She rubbed the back of her hand over her mouth and poked a finger into Jackson's chest. "Mark my spot. I'll be right back. Don't go anywhere."

Then with a deep breath, she grabbed Isabella's hand and dragged her through the doorway to the costume room behind the stage. "Get dressed and saddle up. You're in for a wild ride tonight, if you're lucky."

"I don't know if I can do it." Isabella's body trembled.

"You don't have to." Audrey let out a long sigh. "I don't have to paint the outside of the Ugly Stick and you don't have to earn a wad of cash."

"No." Isabella closed her eyes and pictured Sundance, black as night, standing with his head held high, his raven mane streaming in the wind. She opened her eyes and squared her shoulders. "At five hundred dollars a dance, I can't afford to miss this opportunity."

Audrey pulled her into her arms. "You can do this. It's only eight men. They'll behave, Jackson made them promise."

"Don't worry. I can handle it." Isabella pulled her tank top over her head and tossed it onto a box.

"Let me." Audrey rounded behind her and unhooked her bra.

Her boss's fingers skimming across the skin of her back made Isabella tingle all over. After Audrey and Jackson had practically made love in front of her, Isabella was still a little titillated. Good. She'd use her arousal to prime the pump for her upcoming dance.

"You don't have to stay." Isabella slid her bra straps down her arms and laid the garment over the tank top, pressing her hands to her naked breasts. "The O'Briens will make sure no one gets out of hand."

"But I don't want to leave you alone." Audrey laid a

hand on her arm, turning Isabella to face her. "Are you going to be all right?"

Isabella hugged her boss, disregarding her own nakedness. "Really, I'm okay. I won't fall apart. It's a job. Nothing more." Even if part of her wished it could be.

Audrey's pretty brows furrowed and she set Isabella at arm's length. "If you're sure."

"I am. Now go home." She turned Audrey away and gave her a gentle shove. "I'll feel weird stripping in front of you."

"Uh, honey, you just did." The pretty owner of the saloon laughed. "As if I haven't seen it all. I'm a former stripper, remember? Seen it all before. Even did a woman or two." She tossed a glance over her shoulder, waggling her brows. "If I didn't have Jackson in my life, I might consider making a play for you. You have lovely breasts, by the way." She winked.

Isabella's pussy tightened as an image of a naked Audrey with another naked, faceless woman sprang to mind. Wow...wow. Heat flushed her cheeks. "Go on, before you corrupt me further."

"Ah, sweet, innocent Isabella, you have so much to learn about yourself." Audrey waved. "Libby will be serving at the bar and Greta Sue will be manning the front door. The food is set out, all the boys need is the entertainment. That's you. Break a leg." She turned and tossed a parting comment over her shoulder, "I'm only a phone call away, if you need anything." Then Audrey left.

Isabella stood with her hands over her peaked nipples. A waft of air blew down over her from the air-conditioner ductwork overhead, cooling her heated skin.

You can do this.

Audrey had said she only had to strip down to as much as she felt comfortable.

Isabella stepped out of her cutoffs and panties and slipped into the miniscule thong and bikini top. The cool air now seemed icy, raising goose bumps on her arms.

She added the red-sequined vest and the black chaps and still felt pretty darned naked. If she stripped just the vest and the chaps, that would leave two full dances and the remainder of the first dance with nothing else to do but ride the horse or wiggle around the dance floor. They had a pole she could have incorporated in her routine, but she'd tried several times, unable to make it look natural and sexy. Short of a fireman's slide, she'd just mess it up.

"Are you ready for some action?" Libby's voice called out through the stage curtain.

The men on the other side of the curtain whooped and hollered, whistled and catcalled.

Her music started, her cue to emerge from behind the curtain and take on the task of dancing—for five hundred dollars a pop.

At the last second, panicking like she'd said she wouldn't, Isabella had an idea.

SEAN HAD PACKED his wallet with twenties, determined to get as much out of this bachelorette party as he could. Meaning he wanted to see as much of the beautiful Isabella as she'd let him pay to glimpse. A knot lodged in his chest at the idea of paying her to expose herself to him. At the same time, his cock twitched at the wickedness of giving a female money to show him some skin. He'd never had to pay before, and the idea set his body humming. Who knew he had an inner porn-lover begging to get out?

Hell, he'd tried asking Isabella out, only to be turned down so many times, he'd begun to doubt his own sex appeal. The previous evening he'd asked six other women to dance with him to prove to himself he still had it. Each woman had jumped at the chance.

Why not Isabella?

At the end of the night, he'd left alone. No other woman appealed to him as much as she did. He worried that her stubborn refusal to go out with him actually turned him on and made him want her more. Problem was, he had competition from his brothers. Maybe she was having a hard time choosing.

Sean cracked his knuckles, his back stiffening. Well, he'd just have to show her he was the one for her. Gabe had gotten a step up on him when he'd sneaked back into the Ugly Stick the first night Isabella had ridden the mechanical horse, but Sean was no quitter, having already cornered her in town once. He went after what he wanted with determination and laser focus. He may be younger than Tanner and Gabe, and even Isabella by a year. He made up for his youth in physical strength, maturity and size—he stood at least an inch taller than Tanner and two inches taller than Gabe, a fact that irritated the fire out of both brothers. Not only was he taller, he believed his cock was bigger than his brothers', another fact he took pride in.

They'd argue to their deaths, but Sean knew. He'd seen

his brothers naked on more than one occasion. When Connor Mason had been wooing his sweetie, Charli Sutton, he'd enlisted the three O'Brien brothers to help satisfy Charli's fantasies.

At first, Sean felt weird making love to Connor's woman in front of Connor and his brothers. When Charli had been more than willing, all of the men had focused on pleasuring the woman, not feeling strange about their nakedness or how close they were to one another.

Frankly, ever since Sean and his brothers had been involved in Connor's sexual exploits, he'd been less satisfied one-on-one. One woman with multiple men was damned hot. He and his brothers had agreed on that subject from early on.

Sean stared at the curtain, waiting for Isabella to emerge, thinking about her and the dilemma of choosing between the brothers.

He'd learned that Isabella loved working with horses and being in the outdoors. She was the ideal woman for him and the ranch, if he could convince her to choose him.

The music swelled and still Isabella had not appeared.

Sean leaned forward. Was she injured? Was she hiding behind the curtain, paralyzed with stage fright?

Gabe stood and took a step toward the stage.

Tanner's hand shot out. "Wait." He nodded toward the curtain.

Isabella stepped through, her eyes round, her body...

"What the hell?" Gabe dropped back into his chair, his brow furrowed.

Sean chuckled, then broke out into a full, belly laugh.

Isabella had on several layers of costumes, giving her the appearance of a homeless Vegas act. She glared at Sean, then focused her gaze straight ahead, moving in stilted motions across the stage to the beat of the bump-and-grind music playing on the juke box.

At the edge of the stage, she slipped a leather Dominatrix jacket studded with metal rivets over her shoulders, bent her knees and blew a kiss to Jesse. She let the jacket fall to the tips of her fingers, then flung it to the side of the stage. With a flick, she tossed her long, silky hair over her shoulder and turned her back to the men.

Sean's laughter trickled into a soft chuckle.

"Hey, 'Bella, show us some skin!" one of Jesse's buddies shouted.

Tanner rose from his chair, his fists clenched.

Sean clamped a hand on his brother's arm. "Down, boy. You have to let her dance."

Tanner growled low in his chest and sank into his chair, his brows forming a deep V over his nose.

"I know how you feel. I don't want other men ogling her either." Sean patted his brother's back and pulled a twenty from his wallet. "Maybe we can get the ball rolling with a little encouragement." He stepped away from Tanner. "Don't punch me, bro."

"Does this help?" Sean held out his hand, the twenty dangling from his fingertips.

Isabella's eyes widened. Her body stilled for a moment, then she swished her hips from side to side, finally presenting one to Sean. "Tuck it in where it won't fall out." She rocked her pelvis.

His cock pressing hard against his fly, Sean placed his

hand against her belly and slid the bill against her skin, down into the triangle front of the sequined red thong. When his knuckles brushed against soft, curly hairs, his knees weakened.

Isabella danced away, laughing, her voice adding to the music, swirling all around. She removed a gold lamé scarf and let it drift to the floor.

Sean stood for a moment, captivated by the beauty.

"Hey, move. You're blocking the view!" a voice called out.

Tearing himself away from the stage, Sean returned to his seat and eased down, his jeans so tight, they hurt.

"That gave me a hard-on just watching," Gabe muttered.

Her back to the stage, Isabella slipped a long-sleeved, sheer white blouse halfway down her back and glanced over her shoulder with an exaggerated wink.

"Take it off!" the men shouted, Sean calling out just as loud.

The shirt dropped to her fingers and she spun, flinging it at the leering spectators. Wearing baggy pants that hung low enough around her hips they gave a glimpse of her thong, topped with a sparkling red vest, buttoned in the middle of her cleavage, she danced from one corner of the stage to the other, shimmying. The vest did little to hide her midriff, giving the men a view of smooth skin, tight abs and a sexy belly button.

She dipped her shoulders, leaning toward Jesse, her eyelids sinking low over her beautiful blue-gray eyes.

The shadow between full, rounded breasts made Sean

want to touch, to squeeze, to hold her naked against his skin.

"I'm next." Tanner ripped a bill from the stash in his wallet and leaped from his seat, advancing on the stage as another man did the same.

With a withering glance, Tanner sent the other man scurrying back to his chair.

Isabella spun away and danced back to the edge of the stage. She leaned over, presenting her cleavage. "You know what to do?"

"You bet." Tanner slid the bill into the V.

Sean moaned and shifted in his chair, adjusting his jeans. Having the biggest cock of the brothers proved to be a disadvantage at times like this.

Tanner's fingers lingered in her costume.

Gabe stood, his arms crossing over his chest. "Tanner." He spoke the one word with all the authority of the eldest O'Brien brother.

Tanner jerked his hand back and turned toward the table he shared with his brothers, his cheeks a ruddy red, a frown settling across his forehead.

Isabella straightened, sliding her fingers inside her bikini bra to secure the bill. She winked at Gabe and danced away. She waved toward the baggy pants, her gaze sweeping across the faces of the enraptured men. "More?"

"God, yesss!" Jesse yelled, his eyes glazed, his words slurring to the tune of the amount of alcohol he'd absorbed.

One of his buddies elbowed him in the side. "Hey, you're about to get married."

"I'm getting married, not castrated." Jesse laughed. "My

future wife is the most beautiful woman in the world, but I can appreciate great artwork when I see it. And Isabella is a piece of…art."

"Take it off," Sean whispered.

Another man stood and punched the air with a fist. "Take it off!"

Soon all the men were on their feet, Sean included, each chanting, *Take it off.*

Isabella grabbed the front of the dark, baggy pants she wore and yanked them away, the Velcro strips along the side seams gave and the garment flew to the side of the stage where the jacket lay in a heap.

Beneath the baggy pants, she wore shiny, black, faux-leather chaps over the bright red, sequined thong.

Sean groaned, wishing she'd ride him with those incredibly hot chaps.

The crowd hooted and hollered, stomping their cowboy boots on the wooden floor.

The song faded away and with it, Isabella ducked back behind the curtain.

The three minutes she'd performed had passed fast.

Sean was so hot, he unbuttoned the top button of his crisp white shirt and took a long pull on his cool beer.

"She's got that effect on me too." Gabe loosened a button on his shirt as well, grabbed a bandana from his back pocket and wiped his forehead. "I don't know how much more I can take."

"I don't think baby brother can take much more, either." Tanner nodded toward Jesse.

Jesse waved toward the stage. "What happened to the tradition of the bachelor getting a lap dance?" he yelled.

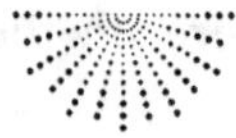

Isabella cringed, dreading what came next. She'd never performed a lap dance, not even in the privacy of her own bedroom with Daniel, or any other man for that matter. In preparation, she'd danced around a chair in her apartment, but she figured it would be a lot different with a man seated in the chair, with long legs and boots to trip over, not to mention hands grabbing while she tried to dance.

She sucked in a deep breath to steady her galloping heartbeat. The last dance wouldn't have been so bad, but having Sean and Tanner touch her skin had set her nerves aflame, especially having had sex with their brother. Her core throbbed, and she worried that if she let them do much more, she'd forget she was there just to dance.

The second song blasted through the speaker system.

Isabella jumped, grabbed some props and dashed for the curtain.

When she stepped out, the men whooped and whistled.

A slow burn worked its way up her neck into her cheeks. Her anxiety receding, she realized she liked this gig more than she'd expected. Dancing half-naked for a small group of men had a liberating effect on her. She'd never felt more powerful or feminine. The tough texture of the riding crop grasped in her fist only added to the Dominatrix part she'd imagined playing.

"Oh, boy! It's lap dance time," a man called out.

"Makes me wish I was the bachelor getting married," another moaned. "I'd like to have me some of that riding my…"

His friend elbowed him in the gut. "Manners, dude."

Isabella swayed to the edge of the stage and waited, her brows raised, her gaze on Sean, Tanner and Gabe. "Can a lady get a lift?"

The three sprang to their feet, each holding out their hands to help her down.

Tanner and Sean reached her first, grabbing a hand to help her off the stage.

Gabe stood in front of her, held out his palm and twirled her into his arms and back out again. "You're beautiful."

Her body warmed as his deep, rich voice coated her like melted chocolate. As much as she wanted to explore more of these three O'Brien men, the youngest awaited the traditional lap dance.

Sean gripped her hand and brought it to his lips. "Later."

Tanner took her other hand and led her to his brother.

"We're not done."

A thrill shivered over her body. Although the hour grew late, the night held more promise than Isabella knew how to handle. She stood in front of the handsome Jesse who would walk down the aisle the next day with his beautiful bride.

His head lolled back, his eyes glazed, a goofy smile sliding across his face. "I hope Ellie won't be upset. Sure hate for her to stand me up at the altar."

Isabella smiled. "I'll be gentle."

As the music swelled, Isabella swayed her hips, losing herself in the rhythm. Jesse looked so much like his brothers, Isabella imagined she was dancing for Gabe, Sean or Tanner, or better yet…all three. She sat in Jesse's lap and turned her back to him, bending to reach for her toes, giving him a full view of her practically naked bottom.

"Spank her, man," his friend shouted.

"Yeah, if you don't, I will," another interjected, laughing.

Isabella chose that moment to glance up.

Sean, Tanner and Gabe stood close, their hands clenched at their sides, their faces set in grim lines, their jeans bulging at the fly. Each man's gaze locked on her exposed ass.

Isabella arched her back, bringing her breasts into view.

The three men sucked in breaths as one, their chests rising and falling as they exhaled.

Oh, yeah, the night could be a lot more interesting, if she chose to seduce all three.

A power surge like none she'd felt before ripped

through Isabella, giving her the courage to ramp up the sex factor and make the lap dance more for the bachelor's brothers than the engaged one, whose lap she occupied. She wiggled her bottom and rose to sit in his lap again, grinding her ass against the rising ridge in his jeans. Even the almost married man couldn't resist a little action.

"You gotta stop that, or I'll be divorced before I make it to the altar." Jesse grabbed her chaps and pushed her toward his brothers. "Dance for my brothers. I'll watch and think of my fiancée."

Isabella stumbled toward Gabe, Tanner and Sean. Tanner caught her, his hands landing around her rib cage beneath the swell of her breasts.

"Let her dance with me. I'll be nice." A sandy-blond-haired man stepped forward, his hands held out toward Isabella.

Jesse shook his head. "No way, Ernie. Cassie claims you have arms like an octopus."

"I'll behave." A dark-haired Hispanic man claimed. "*Por favor*, let her dance for me."

"Mario, you're married. Keep it that way." Jesse grinned up at his brothers. "Besides, my brothers are smitten with the lovely Isabella. I'm curious to see which one she chooses."

Isabella frowned.

"Am I a game to you O'Briens?" She brushed Tanner's hands away and stood with her hands fisted on her hips.

"No." All four brothers spoke at once.

"I just want to take you out. Get to know you," Sean said.

"I want to date you," Gabe said.

"Me too," Tanner added. "Question is why you won't go out with any of us?"

Her hands fell to her sides. Isabella had one good reason for not wanting to go out with them. And it had nothing to do with them, so she shrugged and lied. "I can't decide which one I like best."

Tanner's frown deepened.

Gabe stared at her, eyes narrowed, not uttering a word.

Only Sean whooped. "The rest of you losers can back off. She likes us."

"Let her dance." Jesse stood, pushing his way through his brothers, giving Isabella some space. "This is my last night as a single man. There's nothing I'd like more than to watch my brothers suffer, fighting over one woman. You don't know how good it feels that I'm marrying the woman of my dreams and I'll have her all to myself." He waved toward Isabella. "Dance. Maybe that will help you decide which one of these boneheads you want."

Isabella slipped away from the men and climbed the steps onto the stage, her breath labored. Had her lie been an untruth? Or had it been too close to the truth?

With the music twisting around the thoughts in her mind, she undulated and swayed her way toward the mechanical horse, choosing to ride to ease her troubled and confused thoughts.

She switched on the motor, grabbed the fake mane and swung up onto the fiberglass beast.

As the horse turned and bucked beneath her, Isabella held on, her body moving with the music and the rhythm of the beast. With the men watching, their gazes caressing her from top to bottom, heat rose from her core to spread throughout her body. Moisture pooled in her channel, and each rub against her pussy sent fractured spikes of electricity shooting straight to her center.

The riding crop found its way between her legs, tapping at the triangle of fabric covering her clit. She wanted to strip naked and ride bareback, her slit rubbing against the leather crop.

As the song came to an end, she slid off the mechanical horse and fled behind the curtain, so aroused she didn't know how she'd go on for another dance. And loving every elevated sensation she was feeling.

She leaned against a beam, her hands trembling so badly she dropped the crop to the floor. Isabella slid her fingers over her bare midriff and down into the tiny swatch of material over her pussy, seeking the bundle of nerves buried between her folds.

There. She flicked the bud, sending a pulse of shocks straight to her core. Isabella gasped.

"You all right in here?"

Isabella yanked her hand free of her costume and spun to face the source of the voice.

Libby stood with her head poked through the gap in the curtain, a smile curling the corners of her lips. "The guys are getting restless, but if you want I can stall them for another five minutes with drinks."

"No. I only need a minute. Then you can start the music."

"Will do." Libby's head disappeared, then reappeared. "For what it's worth, you're doing such a good job, you almost made me come. I want to borrow that thong." She winked and withdrew, leaving Isabella alone to gather her wits.

How could she go back out there when all she wanted to do now was to throw her legs open and let each one of the O'Brien men fuck her until she couldn't stand for a week? Her tummy clenched and a heat washed over her pussy. Had she known stripping would generate such and erotic response, she'd have done it years ago.

Her nipples were taut little buttons, poking hard at the bikini bra, her gut knotted, her pussy contracted and her knees wobbled.

On top of all her physical responses, the music started up again.

Isabella moaned, pressing her hands to her breasts, squeezing hard as another flash of desire rocketed through her. Was this what it felt like to have an orgasm?

"Isabella? You coming out?" Libby called.

With little willpower left and too many thoughts of hot, nasty sex crowding her mind, Isabella had to remind herself, once again, why she was there. One more dance would give her another five hundred dollars. No matter how unsteady, how aroused or scared she was, she had to do it.

She stumbled to the curtain and flung it open.

The saloon was empty, only Libby stood at the bar, polishing the shiny wood surface with her cloth. "They all got up and left."

A heavy knot hit the pit of Isabella's gut so hard, she wanted to throw up. "Are they coming back?"

"I think some of them are." Libby grinned. "You're not getting off that easy. Greta Sue is driving the drunk home, but some of them wanted to stay, saying something about wanting their third dance. You want me to start the music over when they come back in?"

She didn't have to, the O'Brien men returned less the groom.

Isabella stood on the stage, motionless.

"You fellas gonna want another drink?" Libby asked.

Gabe shook his head. "You can go home. We're done drinking." His gaze never left Isabella's face.

A shiver rippled across her skin, raising gooseflesh on her arms.

"I'm almost done here, then I'm headed out. Might get home early for once." Libby cast a glance at Isabella. "You want me to stick around to lock up?"

"No," Isabella said. "I have a key. I'll lock up."

Libby gathered her keys and leather jacket, nodding at the O'Brien men. "Don't do anything I wouldn't. Which basically means, have fun." And she left.

"Do you still want me to dance?" Isabella asked from her perch on the stage.

"Dad said he was paying for three," Tanner said, his face set, his dark brown, intense stare focused on her. "We hope you'll stay and earn your pay." His lips softened into a smile.

Isabella's knees weakened. That had to be one of the very few real smiles she'd seen on Tanner. "Of course." *Anything you ask, as long as you smile at me that way.*

Alone with the three men who'd been foremost on her mind, Isabella concentrated on maintaining her footing when her legs wobbled like limp rubber bands.

The music played on. Libby must have lined up several

songs.

Only obligated to dance to one more song, Isabella didn't care. Tanner, Gabe and Sean pulled up seats near the raised stage and sat, waiting for her to begin.

Letting the music fill her body and soul, she closed her eyes and swayed gently, her hips moving in circular motions like Audrey had shown her one day in the storeroom. Isabella crossed her hands over her waist, spreading them over her bare belly, then raising them to clutch the vest buttoned in the middle. She pulled the button free and let the vest fall off her shoulders to the floor.

Cool air caressed her heated skin, but it wasn't enough to extinguish the fire building inside. Isabella wanted to be closer to the men who'd sparked the flame. She reached out her arms.

All three men leaped to their feet. Gabe reached her first, tugging her hand hard enough to pull her off balance.

Isabella fell forward, completely confident Gabe wouldn't let her hit the ground.

He caught her in his arms, sweeping her legs out from under her. After he swung her around once, he set her on her feet, his hands resting on her hips. "You don't have to do anything you don't want to," he whispered against her hair.

"I want this." Her words feathered across his cheek.

"All three of us?" He pulled back, staring down into her eyes.

"Maybe that's what I need."

"Isabella, you're beautiful and the sexiest woman I

know. Don't ever think you're not, because you are. I'm greedy and don't want to share, but…" Gabe held her gaze and at last shrugged. "… For you." His mouth descended to claim hers.

The kiss started out a soft pressure, growing more insistent until Isabella opened her mouth, letting Gabe's tongue slide past her teeth to toy with her own.

A third, strong, male hand caressed her shoulder, sliding down her length to cup her bottom. Tanner leaned in and captured her earlobe, nibbling gently. "You take my breath away."

Gabe pulled her closer until her pelvis fit snugly against his thighs. He pressed a knee between her legs, the coarse fabric of his denim jeans causing a sexy friction against her thong-covered pussy.

Not to be left out, Sean slid his hand up Isabella's rib cage, boldly capturing one of her breasts, his thumb digging beneath the sequined fabric to find and tweak the pointed nipple.

Isabella reached to either side, the backs of her hands sliding over Sean and Tanner's crisply starched cotton shirts, downward to their thick leather belts. She sighed, barely remembering to draw in the next breath.

Gabe's mouth released hers and he leaned back, staring down into her eyes. "Are we overwhelming you?"

Hands stilled on her breast and bottom. "No!" she gasped. Then she slid her hands into the waistbands of Sean's and Tanner's jeans. "I'll let you know if it's too much." Her leg slid up the outside of Gabe's, her cunt rubbing over the top of his thigh. If anything, the thong was too much.

Tanner gripped the string binding one side of the thong and tugged the bow loose. "Sweet mercy."

Gabe untied the other, dragging the tiny scrap of flashy sequins out from under the black chaps.

Sean worked the bow at her neck.

The straps slithered across her collarbone, letting the bra fall forward, her breasts spilling out. He quickly loosened the strap at her back and tossed the garment to the ground. Now all she had on were her chaps and boots.

Feeling decidedly wicked and greedy for having three men where most women settled for one, Isabella pressed her breasts into Gabe's chest, then backed away, tugging at the metal snaps on his shirt. "I don't plan on being the only one naked in this scenario."

"We can fix that." Sean ripped his shirt open, the silver snaps popping open with the force. He tossed the shirt across the stage.

Tanner followed suit, taking it a step further by unbuckling his belt and ripping it free of the loops.

Isabella quivered, her senses on fire. She pushed Gabe's shirt over his shoulders.

He shrugged free of it, the muscles in his chest rippling with every movement.

Isabella reached for his belt buckle, slipping the belt off. The music played on and she danced away from the men, dangling the belt from her hand, letting it slide over her shoulders and down between her breasts.

Sean reached for her. "You're killing us."

She slipped away. "I never finished my lap dance."

All three men sat as one, flies open, chests bare and ready for anything she might do.

Her mind winging ahead, she touched her pussy, the warm juices spurring her to action. "Anyone bring protection?"

Again, all three men moved as one, pulling wallets from back pockets and producing foil packets.

Gabe's fist closed around his condom packet. "Isabella, this isn't part of the bargain."

"No, but it sure would be a bonus." Sean waved his packet. "Mine is ribbed."

Tanner's brow drifted into his usual frown that Isabella found endearing. "What they're trying to say is, no one's forcing you to do anything you don't want to. It's your choice."

Isabella's brows rose. "Oh, I've already chosen."

The men leaned forward.

"Who did you choose?" Sean asked.

Emboldened by her first sense of feeling sexy, Isabella straddled Sean, loving the coarseness of denim against her bottom. "I choose you." She plucked the packet from his fingers and tore it open. Then she scooted back on his knees and unzipped his jeans.

Sean's fully erect cock sprang free. "You're not teasing, are you?"

She leaned forward, her breasts pressing into his hard-muscled chest. "I don't tease." Isabella nipped his ear, then slid the condom over his dick, her fingers lingering, caressing his balls. Her heart sped at Sean's groan. She touched the tip of his cock with her finger. "Now hold that thought."

With more grace than she'd ever known she had, she swung off Sean and straddled Tanner's legs. She pressed a kiss to his furrowed brow. "Don't look so glum. I also choose you." With her hand held out, she wiggled her fingers. "Give."

He placed the package in her palm. "Are you kidding?"

"I thought I covered that with Sean." She slipped his zipper down and scooted off the end of his legs, knelt between his knees and unzipped his jeans.

His cock burst out of the constraining denim. Tanner let out a long breath. "Thank God."

Isabella couldn't resist, she touched her tongue to the rounded head. "Hmm. More later." With deft fingers, she rolled the contraceptive over his prick and moved toward Gabe.

He caught her hands in one of his and yanked her forward.

She toppled, landing on his lap. "Eager, are we?"

He growled. "Damn right." Gabe pressed a hard kiss to her lips and set her back on her feet. With sharp movements, he whipped his dick out of his pants and gripped the foil pouch, ready to tear it open

She nodded, approvingly. "Don't cover yours yet. I have something different in mind for you." With a glance encompassing the three men, excitement ripped through her, making her pussy damp. "Shall we get this show on the road?"

"Hell, yeah!" All three men yelled as one.

Isabella tipped her head. A soft, sensual song filtered through the speakers, echoing across the dance floor. Letting the music guide her, she swayed and undulated, her hands rising above her head and then drifting down her body, flicking the tips of her nipples. She nudged

Gabe's knees apart and sank to all fours. "You boys ready?" She shot a glance at Sean and Tanner.

They sprang to their feet and converged on her and Gabe.

Isabella reached for Gabe's cock, her fingers running the length of the thick, hard shaft, from the tiny hole at the top to the base where his balls nestled in curly hairs. Isabella wiggled her ass as she stuck her tongue out to slide it down Gabe's dick.

"What do you want us to do?" Sean stood beside her, his huge cock jutting out.

Tanner snorted. "If you have to ask, you're too young. Stand back and let the master show you."

"Hey." Sean's hands fisted.

Tanner ignored his brother and dropped to his knees between Isabella's legs and grabbed her hips in his big, coarse hands.

Gabe's fingers threaded into Isabella's hair. "Are you sure you're up to all three of us? I can get rid of these yahoos and we can be alone."

Her stomach fluttered, the thrill of fear creeping in. "No, no. I want all three of you. It's been one of my fantasies." And many of her dreams, lately. And if they were concentrating on pleasing her, she might, just maybe get off, or get close enough to actually fake it.

With her pussy throbbing, her breasts tightened into little peaks, she had to be close. This could be the time she actually came.

Sean dropped to his knees beside her and grasped her breast in his hand, tweaking the nipple between his thumb and forefinger.

Tanner pressed into her, his cock stretching her channel, reminding her of Gabe and their naughty assignation in the costume room a week ago.

Electric currents pulsed through her and she took Gabe's cock into her mouth, sucking at the velvety steel.

Gabe tugged at Isabella's hair, the pressure causing enough pain it made her eyes water and her pussy flush with fluid.

Behind her, Tanner sank deeper until his balls bumped against her.

Isabella's lips tightened around Gabe and she dragged her teeth up his length, softly scraping his skin.

His breath hitched and he stilled, his grip on her hair tightening. "Careful."

She released his cock and licked it. "Always." Again, she sucked him into her mouth, loving the warm muskiness of his skin.

Gabe surged upward, pushing her head down as his cock slid all the way in, until it bumped against the back of her throat.

Behind her, Tanner had settled into a rhythm, driving in and out of her, his pace increasing with each thrust.

Sean massaged her breast, pinching her nipples until she gasped. "Look, you can't be getting much out of this. Let me in there." He flopped onto his back and scooted his legs between Gabe's and under the chair, positioning his head beneath Isabella's pussy.

When Sean's tongue touched her clit, fire singed her veins, her molten blood winging its way throughout her body, pooling at her core.

Hundreds of fingers of flame licked at her nerve

endings, making her jerk, her muscles spasm and her pussy clench around Tanner's cock.

Unable to catch her breath, she paused, her mouth halfway down Gabe's shaft.

Tingles started in her toes and spread, consuming her like a tsunami, engulfing her in a kaleidoscope of brightly colored sensations.

She gasped, her mouth leaving Gabe's dick, her fingernails digging into his thighs. "Oh, God!" Isabella closed her eyes, feelings she'd never experienced washing over her, immobilizing her in wave upon wave of shocks.

Sean touched her again, his tongue swirling around her clit.

"Stop!" she cried. "I'm going to die. Please, stop."

His tongue stilled against the most sensitive spot and remained.

Isabella rode the wave until she collapsed, her body dropping onto Sean. Tanner slipped free, his cock flagging. "You've killed me. I can't move."

Gabe chuckled and reached down to gather her into his arms.

Sean held on to her thigh. "No, leave her there. She feels pretty darned good."

Isabella could only lie there, completely numb, her insides pulsing, the only indication she hadn't died and gone to heaven. Her cheek nudged Sean's cock. "My God, you're huge," she muttered.

Her core tightened. Maybe she wasn't as dead as she'd thought. "I'm okay." She pushed to her hands and knees and swung her leg over Sean.

Gabe stood, took her hand and pulled her into his arms. "You had one hell of an orgasm."

A smile spread across her face, joy filling her heart. "I did, didn't I?"

"Wanna go for another?" Sean stood, brushing the dust off his jeans. "I'm still sheathed and we can change things up to keep it interesting."

Gabe glared at Sean. "Give the gal a break."

"No." Isabella turned into Sean's arms, eager to relive the power of a real honest-to-goodness, holy-cow orgasm. "Show me whatcha got."

"Yeehaw!" Sean grabbed her thighs and hiked her up, wrapping her legs around his waist. "Gabe, you wanna make use of that condom, or are ya gonna stand there with your mouth open, catching flies?"

Sean didn't waste time, he thrust into her. "Damn, woman, you're hot."

Tanner peeled the condom from his cock, a smile quirking at the corners of his lips. "Tell me about it."

Isabella laughed. "That's a good thing, right?"

"You bet." His hands grasping her ass, Sean raised and lowered her, working up to a rhythm. "You about ready there, big brother?"

Gabe grunted behind Isabella. "Yeah."

"Okay." Sean slid free of Isabella's pussy.

"Wait, you're still hard. We're not done," Isabella's legs tightened around Sean.

"No, we're not done." Sean grinned. "Things are about to get more interesting." He nodded to Gabe behind her. "Go for it."

Gabe's fingers slid down the crease of Isabella's ass to the tight little hole of her anus.

Isabella's heart skipped a beat, her breath catching and holding. "What are you about to do?"

His finger slid into her.

The air whooshed out of Isabella's lungs. "Oh my God." She clutched Sean's shoulders.

Sean stared down into her eyes. "Okay so far?"

She nodded, her eyes wide. "Y-yes." Amazingly, she was eager for more.

Gabe's finger left her anus and his cock pressed the entrance.

"You're not going to…" Isabella's gut clenched and she squeezed shut her eyes as Gabe eased into her. "Oh, my. Oh, my… Oh…" She dragged in a shallow breath, then another. The pain subsided and the pressure of Gabe's cock in her ass seemed more natural.

Sean loosened his hold on her thighs and eased her down until the head of his cock prodded her pussy. "Ready?"

"Two?" She gulped. "At once?"

Tanner laughed. "Babe, you will never be the same. I only wish I was a part of it."

"Come here." She waved him closer and grabbed his naked dick, then nodded. "Ready."

With Gabe's cock in one end, Sean's cock sliding into her cunt, her hand gripping Tanner, Isabella couldn't think, breathe or move. Tanner cupped one of her breasts and leaned close to her ear. "Ride it, sweetheart."

And she did.

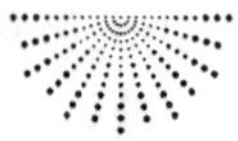

CHAPTER SIX

Isabella slept until noon after a fitful night in which all three O'Brien brothers played a big part in keeping her from the rest she needed. She'd never had erotic dreams before she'd met the O'Briens, nor had she considered multiple sex partners in real life, or her most sordid sensual imaginings, until recently.

But what they'd done in the Ugly Stick Saloon was stuff fantasies were made of.

And her dreams… Whew!

All three men had been in her dreams, in her bed at one time, each trying to win her over by performing lewd and wonderfully lascivious deeds on her body, touching her in places she'd only heard about or watched in the occasional porn movie.

The T-shirt she'd worn to bed lay crumpled on the floor, the sheets had been shoved to the bottom of the bed and she'd awakened to find her legs wrapped around a pillow, her pussy throbbing, her mind and body humming with the images of the three men lying naked beside, beneath and over her.

Her nipples remained puckered from the dream-licking they'd taken and her cunt throbbed, still aching from all the times she'd been fucked by one brother after the other.

Isabella lay back for a long moment, letting the sun shining through the window warm her bare skin. Her hand slid down her ribs toward her belly and lower. She threaded her fingers into the hairs guarding her clit, riding the wave of desire left over from the aftermath of her disturbed slumber.

What would it feel like to have all three O'Brien men in her bed, not in a saloon?

Isabella closed her eyes, sliding a finger between her folds, envisioning Gabe licking her there, while Tanner with his brooding eyes and huge, thick cock, nudged from behind. Sean would be lying beside her thumbing her nipples, sucking them deep into his mouth, bragging that his cock was bigger than his brothers'. When they were done, he'd prove his bragging held merit.

A moan rose from Isabella's throat. When she flicked her clit with the tip of her finger, her body tensed, her back arching off the mattress.

Raw hunger washed over her, wave after wave of electrical tingles shooting through every nerve in her body, burning a path straight to her core.

Her finger dipped into her pussy, coming out drenched in the honey of her desire. She swept it to the bundle of nerves, slathering the juices over and over.

A warm tongue, strong, thick fingers sliding in and out

of her pussy, broad shoulders pressing against her inner thighs…

Yes. Right there.

Another flick and she stilled, her body tightening as a sensation so intense rocketed her up and over the threshold she thought unattainable.

Isabella held her breath, riding the surge to the end when she collapsed against the sheet.

Her eyes widened.

For the first time in years, she'd given herself an orgasm, the feeling so powerful it left her body trembling.

And she'd done it by herself on the tail-end of an explosive night followed by a dream about the three handsome cowboys that had shown her what put the "O" in orgasm.

Her doorbell rang, startling her out of her sex-induced euphoria.

She leaped out of the bed, snatching up her discarded T-shirt and a pair of shorts.

Halfway to the door, dragging on her clothes, the doorbell rang again and Isabella tripped over her shorts and almost fell.

By the time she reached the door, she'd earned a bruise and was breathing hard, her body still warm and tingly from masturbation.

The doorbell rang again.

Isabella grabbed the knob and jerked the door open. "Where's the damned fire?"

Gabe O'Brien, holding a bunch of wildflowers, smiled. "No fire, just me."

Her first impulse was to yank Gabe into the house,

strip the clothes off his back and make love to him on the cool tile floor.

A warm, Texas wind wafted through the doorway, bringing with it the dry scent of dust, reminding Isabella of the last time she'd made love to Daniel. The day they'd split—the same day he'd fired her.

She squelched the urge to jump Gabe's bones. No matter how good he'd been in her dreams, she was raw and a little shy after having achieved the big "O" with the three O'Briens. "What do you want?"

"I want to take you out…alone."

Fear knotted her belly. *Maybe all three, but not just one. Not yet.* "I'm not sure it's a good idea. Last night…was… well…I don't know." *Magical. The sexual highlight of my life. Incredibly insane?* Her gaze shot to his, her cheeks burning as if the man could read her lurid thoughts.

"Okay, let's not call it a date. It's an outing."

"What's the difference?" She crossed her arms, refusing to relieve him of the wildflowers no matter how touching. Isabella much preferred wild to the hothouse variety.

"I promise not to make a pass or anything like I would on a regular date. I just want to take you somewhere I know you'll enjoy."

Her eyes narrowed. "I have to work this evening."

"I'll only take a couple hours of your time." He drew an X over his chest and held his fingers up in a poor attempt at a scout's salute. "Promise."

His face appeared so open and honest, his eyes wide and hopeful. "Please, take a chance. You won't regret it."

Her frown deepening, Isabella tried to hold on to her

resistance, but failed miserably. "Fine." She glanced down at her rumpled T-shirt and threadbare shorts. "Is what I have on good enough?"

His gaze slipped over her from top to toe, a smile curving his lips. "It's more than good enough, if we were staying here. But we're not. Get some jeans and cowboy boots on. If you have a hat, that would be a good idea as well." He glanced up. "No clouds in the sky, which means the sun's gonna be hot today."

"Oh, you mean outing as in outside." She hesitated. "I don't know. I'm really tired." *From having sex with you and your brothers.* More heat suffused her cheeks.

"Please."

When he put it like that, with soulful green eyes, her hand dropped from the doorknob. "Okay, then. Give me a minute to pull myself together." She turned, leaving him standing in the open doorway. "You might as well come in."

Isabella entered her bedroom and rifled through her closet for her best pair of jeans and a white ribbed-knit T-shirt that fit over her curves like a second skin. She brushed her hair, pulling it straight back from her face in a ponytail.

"Nice place," Gabe called out. "What do you call the decor? Country?"

"Thrift shop special." Isabella emerged from her bedroom, carrying her cowboy boots and a pair of socks. "I'm not very girly. I go more for functional." She sat on the old floral couch Audrey had insisted she take, claiming she had another on order and didn't have room for two in her little cottage.

Isabella suspected Audrey hadn't had another couch on order until she'd moved the pretty floral one into Isabella's apartment. It had been her first piece of furniture in her apartment and functioned as a bed until she'd found an inexpensive mattress and box springs at the warehouse store in Austin.

"I particularly like the pictures."

A lump formed in Isabella's throat. She bent to tug on her socks, fighting back a rush of tears.

"This is you, isn't it?" He pointed to a picture of her standing beside Sundance, the jockey, Daniel and his mother Margaret in the winners' circle at the Oaklawn Race Track.

Sundance had won his very first race, his future bright and Isabella had been on top of the world, having been included as part of the team that had resulted in the win.

"Yeah, that's me."

Gabe frowned and leaned closer to the photo. "Is this your old boss and her son?"

"Yes." Isabella tugged her boots on and stood.

"Do you still have feelings for him?"

"Oh, hell no. It's the only picture of Sundance I own."

"Who's Sundance?"

"The horse." She straightened. "Are we going? I need to be back in exactly three hours."

"Right." Gabe grinned and motioned to her head. "Hat?"

Isabella opened the hall closet and retrieved her cowboy hat from the shelf, clapping it on her head. "Ready." She gathered her purse and keys, opened the front door and waited for Gabe to exit.

As he passed Isabella, he paused and leaned close. "Anyone ever tell you that you're hot in jeans and cowboy boots?"

Warmth spread over her skin and swelled in her heart. Daniel had never complimented her when she was wearing her work clothes. And though she had on her best jeans, they were just jeans, the cowboy boots worn and still dusty.

She snorted softly. "Liar."

He captured her chin in his fingers and tipped her face upward. "I don't lie." He dropped a kiss on her lips.

The action was too brief, making Isabella wish for more.

Gabe sauntered away before she could do anything about it.

Just as well.

"You promised you wouldn't try anything," she called out after him.

"I did," he said without turning around.

"What do you call that?" she demanded.

"What?" He glanced over his shoulder, his eyes wide and all innocent-like.

"That…that…" She flung out her hands and stomped past him. "Oh, never mind."

"We can go in my truck."

Isabella rattled her keys. "I'll take my own, thank you."

He shrugged. "Suit yourself."

"I will."

While Gabe strode toward his shiny white pickup truck, Isabella climbed into her rattle-trap pickup that her dad had bought new twenty years ago. Besides photographs, the truck was the only thing she had left that had belonged to her father. She wouldn't part with it for all the money in the world.

Gabe backed out of the driveway and onto the street, leading the way to wherever he had in mind.

Isabella fell in behind him, wondering what had possessed her to go along and glad she had the alone time to pull herself together.

Every one of the O'Brien men had trouble written all over their handsome faces and bodies. After the previous night's performance…Isabella knew she could be in too deep.

She spent the drive time drilling it into her head that handsome men were no good. Hadn't Daniel taught her that lesson?

The devil on her shoulder argued, *Even handsome men who can make you come?*

She forced herself to relive her last day on the Circle C Ranch.

Daniel had used the excuse that he wanted her to ride with him out on the property to check on the horses grazing the north forty.

Isabella should have recognized it as a ruse.

Once out in the north pasture, Daniel had stopped the engine and leaned across the seat to kiss her.

His lips had been dry, the kiss short and Daniel had been in a hurry to get her out of her clothes and into the bed of the truck.

Isabella had gone along with his plan, while secretly going through all the work she had waiting for her when they returned to the horse barn.

Daniel spread a thin blanket over the hard metal truck bed, lay down beside her naked body and ran his fingers down to the apex of her thighs, seeking the center of her folds. For all of approximately two minutes, he had strummed her clit. He hadn't bothered to moisten his efforts, his dry finger rubbing her sensitive parts until they stung.

Isabella had tried to get there, to find that elusive spot, to rise to the occasion, but no matter what fantasies she'd envisioned, mental coaching or prayers to the sex gods, she just couldn't.

When Isabella had shown no signs of climaxing, Daniel muttered a curse, dropped his drawers and fucked her. Two minutes later he rolled off her, zipped his jeans and climbed out of the truck bed.

Isabella had collected her clothing, mentally castigating herself for her failure to come. She'd climbed into the passenger seat and buckled her seatbelt, her heart squeezing in her chest. Why couldn't she come? She'd loved Daniel, didn't she? They'd spent a lot of time together with the horses. He'd been very attentive and had made love to her over and over. Surely that was love.

"Look, Isabella. I can't keep doing it with a woman who won't even respond to my efforts."

She'd stared across at him, her mouth dropping open. Doing it? "It's not as if I'm holding out on you. I try."

"Well, you're not cutting it." He shifted into drive and sped across the dry ground toward the ranch house. "I've had enough. We're done."

Isabella had straightened her shoulders and stared

ahead, gripping the armrest on the door to steady herself on the bumpy ride. "You don't want to see me anymore?"

"That's what *we're done* generally means."

"What about my job?" Her chest tightened. The man was dumping her and all she could think about was her job. That should have told her something. "You'll see me every day."

"What part of *we're done* don't you understand?" Daniel's lip had curled on one side. The same look he had when he was going to say something ugly…to someone else. Not her. "Let me make it plain enough for you." He'd stared across the cab at her. "You're done, finished, fired."

Her mouth hung open, the wind knocked out of her lungs. For a second she had to tell herself to breathe. She'd struggled to retain control as her world spun around her. "All because I can't have an orgasm with you?"

"We obviously don't click and I need more from a woman than just a horse trainer."

"Can't I stay on and just be an employee?"

He shook his head. "You know it'll never work for us to break up and you to still be around. You have to go."

Her fingers dug into the truck's armrest as her life fell to pieces. "What about Sundance?"

"What about him?" Daniel frowned.

"I'm the only one who can get him to perform."

"He'll have to learn to get along with one of the other handlers."

"But—"

"It's over, Izzy."

Isabella had bitten down hard on her tongue. She hated being called Izzy. And she hated even more that she'd never see Sundance again, once she left the Circle C Ranch. "You're sure that's the way you want it?" she'd asked one last time, knowing the answer.

"Yeah, it has to be that way."

In the course of the day, she'd lost her job, her home and the horse she'd nurtured and cared for. All because she couldn't get off with the boss's son.

Lost in the past, Isabella almost rammed into the back of Gabe's pickup when he turned off the highway and passed through the gates of the Rockin' O Ranch.

What the hell?

Her foot let off the accelerator and the distance increased between hers and Gabe's trucks.

Pressure descended on her chest, making her want to turn and drive away. She hadn't been on a ranch since she'd been escorted off the Circle C. An overwhelming flood of longing swept over her. Her fingers gripped the steering wheel to keep them from shaking.

Gabe's brake lights flashed, bringing Isabella back to her senses. She stomped her foot to the accelerator, catching up to the infuriating cowboy.

Even if she didn't stay, it would be rude to turn around without an explanation.

As she passed by a paddock with several quarter horses running alongside the fence, she bit down on her bottom lip to keep it from trembling.

God, she missed living on a ranch, being surrounded by animals and the scent of hay and manure.

Some girls would find that disgusting. Not this girl. She loved the earthiness, the hard work and the varying personalities of horses and ranch hands.

By the time she pulled up in the barnyard behind Gabe, she'd gathered her wits, took a deep breath and got out.

When Gabe joined her, she blurted out, "I can't stay. I need to go to work."

"You have at least three hours." Gabe took her hand. "Yes, you can." He tugged her toward the barn.

She dug her heels into the dirt. "I remember, I have to iron my clothes for tonight."

"You don't iron and it's Ladies' Night at the Ugly Stick Saloon. The customers won't be looking at you anyway. They'll be looking at the male strippers." His brows rose. "Any other excuses you'd like to try?"

Out of reasons why she shouldn't be there, she let him lead her into the shadowy interior of the barn. Isabella inhaled deeply, the aroma of hay and sweet feed bringing back memories of her father and mother and growing up on a small farm in the Texas Hill Country. Her father had worked in construction during the day and tended a small herd of cattle before and after work.

Isabella's mother had taken care of the house and garden while Isabella cared for the only horse they owned. She brushed, fed and exercised Sassy, forming a bond with the horse that lasted even after the horse died of old age. Her love of horses had only grown with time. On her twenty-second birthday, her father had gifted her with a thoroughbred colt. Sundance.

"I don't know about you, but I could use a little fresh air and exercise." Gabe smiled. "I thought we'd go for a ride." He led a dappled gray mare from one of the stalls and tied her lead to a ring on the wall.

Tears welled in Isabella's eyes. The horse had perfect conformation, her bones delicate and strong, and she was so beautiful. A lump formed in Isabella's belly. "I don't think—"

"You'd be doing Stormy a favor." Gabe grabbed a blanket and saddle from the tack room and returned. "We haven't had time to get her out much. She loves to race across the meadows."

As Gabe approached with the saddle, Stormy's ears perked and she whinnied.

The sound brought a surge of joy and longing to Isabella's chest. She leaned toward the horse, her hand reaching out to run down the mare's smooth neck. "She's so excited."

"She loves getting out. Really, you'd be doing her a big favor."

Wavering, Isabella sighed. "I wouldn't want to disappoint her."

"Hear that, Stormy?" Gabe settled the gear on the horse's back. "You're going for a ride with the pretty lady."

Stormy tossed her head.

Isabella laughed, taking over the chore of saddling the mare. She cinched the girth and adjusted the stirrups to fit her legs.

"Meet Drago." Gabe led a black stallion out of the stall at the end.

Isabella's heart stopped, her breath lodging in her throat. For a moment, Isabella's vision wavered.

"Isabella?" He stopped in front of her. "Are you okay?"

She shook her head to clear her vision. Drago wasn't

Sundance. She hadn't seen a ghost and she wasn't going crazy. "I'm fine."

"Are you sure?"

"Yes."

He handed her a bridle and slipped one over his horse's nose, buckling it in place.

Isabella finished a moment after Gabe. She gathered Stormy's reins and led her through the barn door out into the sunshine.

A light breeze lifted the tendrils from the back of Isabella's neck, taunting her with the promise of wind in her hair while flying across the ground on the back of the pretty mare. She swung up into the saddle and waited.

Gabe emerged from the barn, adjusted the girth on his horse and led Drago across the yard to a gate. He opened it wide and walked the stallion through.

When Isabella passed through the gate, Gabe latched it behind them and climbed up into his saddle. He glanced around at the sound of an approaching vehicle, his brows coming together. "Ready?"

Isabella glanced toward the sound, her hands tightening on the reins, the thought of Tanner and Sean joining them sending ripples of excitement skittering across her nerves. "Don't you want to wait and see who's driving up?"

"Nope." He reined his horse in a one-eighty. "Race ya to the oak tree at the top of the rise."

Isabella forgot about the oncoming vehicle. Giving the horse the slightest nudge with her boot heels, Isabella held on.

Stormy rocketed forward, kicking up grass and dirt in her wake.

Not to be outdone, Drago whinnied behind her, his hooves pounding against the ground.

With the wind whipping her ponytail, her hat hanging around her neck by the string, Isabella hadn't felt this carefree in a long time. She laughed out loud, a shiver of anticipation and desire swelling inside. She reveled in the open air, the scent of fresh hay, and the power of bunching and flexing muscles beneath her. The combination made her believe she could conquer anything.

Including achieving an orgasm with a man like Gabe O'Brien.

CHAPTER SEVEN

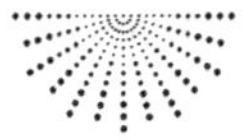

Gabe gave Drago his head, urging him faster.

The stallion easily passed the smaller mare and moved ahead, the competitive streak hard to subdue in man or beast.

Once they reached the tree on the hill, Gabe would drop over the other side and out of sight of the barn. If he was not mistaken, Sean and Tanner had been in the vehicle they'd heard approaching the barn. Damn, they'd finished their errands in town much quicker than he'd anticipated. If they caught wind of Gabe taking Isabella out on the ranch, they'd want to tag along.

Brothers interrupting wasn't in the plan Gabe had in mind.

The hot Texas sun beat down on his back, bringing a smile to Gabe's face. Also part of his plan. Later.

As he neared the top of the hill and the lone, gnarled live oak providing the only shade in the vicinity, he reined in and waited for Stormy and her rider to catch up, which didn't take long.

They arrived shortly after Drago halted.

Isabella's face shone, her wind-kissed cheeks aglow, eyes alight, sparkling in the sunshine. God, she was beautiful.

Gabe's chest swelled. He wanted to pull her into his arms and hold her, to press kisses to her apple cheeks, the curve of her breasts and…

Patience.

Isabella was like a skittish colt, needing much control and coaxing to bring her out of whatever hellish shell she'd wrapped herself in that kept her from committing to one man.

Gabe smiled at her. "Come on. I want to show you a special place."

"Lead on. Stormy and I are along for the ride." She leaned over, rubbing the horse's neck. "She's fast and beautiful." Her gray eyes shadowed, the smile on her lips slipping. As quick as hitting a light switch, her sunny expression faded into the shadows of the live oak.

"Is something wrong?" Gabe asked.

"No. Nothing." She smiled, her lips tight.

If Gabe was not mistaken, she forced the smile, and not very convincingly.

He had his work cut out for him to learn what made her lose the happiness she'd begun the ride with.

Setting off at a more sedate pace, he led the way, dropping over the ridge of the hill into a wide, green valley and rising up another hill beyond. Rolling plains of hayfields stretched as far as he could see. By the time he got close to their destination, the heat of the day bore down on them.

A thin sheen of perspiration gave Isabella's face a warm, healthy glow. She'd settled her cowboy hat on her head, the shade hiding her expressive blue-gray eyes.

As they topped yet another rise, Gabe paused and waited for Isabella to move up beside him. He wanted to see her face when she gazed down at the little valley.

Isabella reined in next to him, a small frown wrinkling her brow. "Why are we stop—" Her gaze panned the valley below, her eyes widening. "It's beautiful," she whispered.

Gabe's heart squeezed. He felt the same way every time he stared down at the valley with the sparkling clear stream running through, surrounded by old-growth live oaks, willows and cypress trees.

Drago and Stormy pranced, tossing their heads.

"I think they're thirsty." Gabe cast a glance at Isabella. "How about you?"

Isabella tugged at her shirt. "I could stand to cool off in the shade."

"We can do better than that." Gabe gave the stallion his head.

The stallion bolted forward, charging down the hill toward the banks of the creek.

A quick glance over his shoulder made Gabe smile.

Isabella wasn't far behind. She was fearless on horseback.

When they reached the creek, Gabe pulled Drago to a halt and dropped to the ground.

Stormy arrived beside him, her rider laughing.

By the time Gabe reached up to help Isabella out of the saddle, she'd jumped to the ground.

Able and independent. Gabe liked that in a woman. Only it didn't give him a chance to touch her. And boy, he wanted to touch her so badly it hurt.

After watering the horses, Gabe tied them to a tree.

He stripped off his shirt and hung it over a mountain laurel bush.

Isabella paused from dipping her hand in the water and glanced up. "What are you doing?"

He grinned. "I don't know about you, but I'm hot. I'm going in to cool off. Join me if you want."

"I didn't bring a swimsuit."

"Then we're even." His smile broadened. "Neither did I."

She frowned. "I thought you said you wouldn't try anything."

"I'm not trying anything. Just going for a swim." He shucked his boots and stripped his jeans down his legs. In two long strides, he launched himself into the wide, clear water.

Isabella stood like a fool with her mouth gaping open.

When Gabe had taken off his clothing, instead of looking away, Isabella had watched with abject fascination, unable to tear her gaze away from all the naked muscles gleaming in the dappled light shining through the trees.

Holy horses! Last night had been a blur, she'd seen his chest and his cock, but the altogether was even more impressive. He was built like a god…hell, he was hung like a…

Isabella swallowed hard, her pussy clenching, throbbing, remembering her shameless behavior at the saloon the night before.

Gabe surfaced, flung back his head and shouted, "Feels great! Are you coming in?"

Isabella hesitated, though her hands rose to the hem of her shirt as though they had minds of their own. What was she thinking? Skinny-dipping with Gabe? It could only lead to one thing.

Shivers of anticipation shimmied across her arms, raising gooseflesh on her heated skin. What if he wanted to pleasure her? What if she couldn't get off without his brothers to help? Would he think any less of her?

"I promise not to touch you, if that's what you want," he called out, floating on his back, his dick rising straight out of the water.

"I'll take you up on that promise." Before her feet got cold, she ripped her shirt over her head, toed off her boots and shimmied out of her jeans and panties. In seconds, she dove into the cool water.

She rose to the surface, laughing, her heart lighter than it had been in a long time. "You're right. It feels great."

Gabe maintained his distance.

Warmth filled her chest and spread lower. Yet a twinge of self-doubt lingered. Would he be judging her attributes? Would she come up short?

The man had enough manners to allow her to adjust to the water temperature and to being alone with a naked man in a pool. Daniel would have been all over her.

Not Gabe.

Hmm. What if she wanted him to be all over her? Her sexual curiosity stormed every cell in her body, and Isabella pushed aside her insecurities and ducked beneath the surface. She kicked off the bottom, swam hard and fast toward Gabe, grabbed his ankle and yanked him under. So what if she couldn't get off. Today wasn't forever. At least Gabe could have a little fun with her and she could enjoy sex without coming. It wasn't all about her having an orgasm.

TANNER RACED ACROSS THE FIELDS, urging his horse faster.

His brother, Sean, followed, leaning low over his bay gelding's jet-black mane.

Damn Gabe.

Their father had met them at the barn, a grin on his face. "I see Gabe has the jump on you boys."

They'd been unloading the supplies and sacks of grain Gabe had sent them to purchase, insisting they go all the way over to the feed store in Hole in the Wall instead of their usual trip to Temptation. He'd said he'd read they were having a sale. When they'd arrived, the feed store clerk had stared at Tanner like he'd grown a second head. What sale?

Now he understood why Gabe had sent them across to the next county. He'd bought enough time to get Isabella out to the ranch...alone. Screw that. How was Tanner supposed to woo the pretty waitress if Gabe stayed one step ahead?

Isabella deserved a chance to get to know all three of

them. Then she could choose which one she'd rather be with.

After last night, Tanner was even more determined to win over the beautiful Isabella.

Tanner intended to make sure she got to know him as much as she got to know Gabe. He had a good idea where they'd end up, riding with the temperatures in the nineties.

The creek.

Sun beat down on him, reminding him that the heat would take it out of the horses at the pace they'd set. Tanner slowed his mare to a trot, himself chomping at the bit, wishing he'd opted for the four-wheeler instead. At least then he could have roared across the pasture without worrying about the animals.

Sean rode up beside Tanner. "I can't believe Gabe would go behind our backs and take Isabella out without us."

"She doesn't belong to us." Though Tanner wished she did. God, last night… All three of them making love to her… His cock twitched, hardening beneath the denim.

"I thought she'd made it clear, she wanted all of us," Sean continued.

"We don't know what exactly she wants. That could have been for just last night. Like trying all the candy in the box until she finds the one she likes best."

"Shoot." Sean removed his cowboy hat and scrubbed his arm across his forehead. "And I thought… Oh hell. I don't know what I thought. Once she removed her bikini, my brain quit functioning."

Tanner laughed. "And your dick did your thinkin' for you?"

Sean scowled. "I wouldn't be talking. Seems yours was doin' it for you too."

"And Gabe's was thinkin' for him. That woman had us all tied in knots."

"In a good way, you gotta admit." Sean grinned. He didn't stay mad for long. "I'd go for it again. I don't mind sharing, as long as *she's* happy. Makes me real hot."

Tanner's brows narrowed. "I'm not so sure *I* want to share her."

"Even if it's the way *she* wants it?"

Tanner's hand tightened on the reins and his mare danced to the side. "Although what we did last night was…well…incredible…I want her to myself."

Sean shook his head. "Maybe one isn't enough for her. Ever think of that?"

"*I* could be enough for her, if she'd give me a chance to prove it." Tanner didn't like the way this conversation was going. They all needed a woman, or so their father said. The old man wanted grandchildren, and plenty of them. Hell, Tanner wanted a kid or two. Someday.

If all three of them wanted Isabella, someone was bound to lose out. She'd ultimately choose one.

Tanner's chest tightened. Would he step aside if she refused to make a decision? Just because he didn't want to share?

What if there was truth in what Sean was saying?

His thoughts churned on the idea as they crossed another pasture light green with knee-high Bermuda hay swaying in the warm breeze.

What if Isabella didn't want to choose? If they forced her to, would she leave them all?

Holy hell. Tanner didn't like sharing his woman with other men, but he would be less hesitant if the other men were his brothers. They loved each other and would do anything to protect what was theirs. Hell, they'd shared a woman before Isabella.

Though that had been a bit different. None of them had been romantically interested in Charli Sutton. Sure she was sexy, and making love to her with their friend, Connor Mason, had been exciting. But now that they'd discovered Isabella, the woman who'd been under their noses all along… Tanner couldn't imagine making love to anyone else—with or without his brothers in the picture.

But he might consider putting a fist in Gabe's face for sending them on a snipe hunt.

As he topped the last hill, he reined in his horse. Sean came to a halt beside him.

"Damn." Sean whistled. "The man works fast. He's got her in the pool."

Tanner's jaw tightened. "And she's naked." He dug his heels into his mare's flanks, sending the horse down the hill, charging toward the creek.

SEAN WHOOPED BEHIND TANNER, his horse's hooves pounding to keep up. From the top of the hill, he could see Gabe tossing Isabella into the air, water glistening on her pale skin. Oh, yeah. He wanted in on that action.

Unlike his middle brother, Sean didn't care if he shared Isabella with his siblings. As long as she had some love left in her for him. After spending time with her at the saloon, walking her home, flirting with her over the bar and the occasional dance she graced him with, he was convinced, she was the one for him.

She liked horses. Sean liked horses. She loved ranch life. Sean couldn't imagine living anywhere else. Isabella believed in family and taking care of the people and critters she loved. What more could a cowboy ask for in the woman he planned to spend the rest of his life with?

If sharing her with his brothers made Isabella happy and more fulfilled, that was fine by him. Anything to keep her in the family.

Tanner beat him to the edge of the pool, pulling up so sharply, his mare reared and whinnied, announcing their arrival better than any shout-out.

Gabe and Isabella had just surfaced, rivulets of water running down their faces, necks and shoulders.

Isabella's breasts bobbed near the surface, shining and wet—so luscious, they looked like ripe melons to be sucked on.

Sean was out of the saddle before his gelding came to a full stop. "Hey, no fair. You didn't wait for us."

Gabe glared. "Because you weren't invited."

Sean's brows rose. "We'll leave if Isabella wants us to."

"Speak for yourself," Tanner muttered. "I'm not going anywhere."

Sean turned the full force of his killer smile on Isabella. "What's it to be? Do you want us to leave the two of you alone?"

Isabella's cheeks reddened and she glanced at Gabe, her hands rising to cover her naked breasts.

Gabe sighed. "It really is your choice."

"I don't want to start a fight among your brothers," she said.

"Then tell us what you really want, sweetheart," Sean urged. "We're big boys. We can take it."

The pink in her cheeks darkened and she shot another sideways glance at Gabe, then Tanner and Sean. "You won't be mad?"

Sean raised a hand. "I promise."

Tanner dropped down out of his saddle and nodded. "Me too."

Gabe frowned. "Same."

She gulped, the muscles working in her throat.

Sean held his breath.

Tanner's fists tightened.

Even Gabe froze, awaiting Isabella's response.

"I want all three of you." She straightened, letting her hands fall away from her breasts, her chin tilting up. "Does that make me bad?"

Sean laughed. "Only the best kind of bad there is. Maybe a little greedy too, but sexy as hell." He tore open his shirt, tossing it to the ground. Hopping on one foot, he removed a boot and chucked it.

Tanner stood to the side.

"You're not gonna get a better offer, Tanner," Sean muttered. "Show the woman some love."

His scowl slowly dissipating, Tanner reached for the buttons on his shirt. "I guess it's okay."

"Damn right it is." Sean stepped out of his jeans and dove into the pool, the cool water having little effect on taming his arousal. He swam to Isabella and pulled her into his arms, kissing her soundly. "That's more like it. Come on, Tanner, don't take all day."

A loud splash sent a spray of water crashing into him, and Tanner knocked him over. Sean took Isabella with him, submerging in the refreshing pool.

When he came up, he shouted, joy filling his heart.

"Am I the only one who thinks this pool is crowded?" Gabe mumbled.

"No." Tanner crossed his arms.

ISABELLA PUSHED BACK her dripping hair from her face. She had been afraid of this. By the way Tanner and Gabe were glaring at each other, her own selfishness was causing a rift between the brothers. "Leave, if it bothers any of you. Or better yet, I'll leave." She pushed through the water, headed for shore, her heart hammering against her ribs, a sick feeling settling in the pit of her gut, shame flushing her naked body.

"No, baby. Please…don't go." Sean cut her off, his hands settling on her arm, work-roughened fingers curling around her gently. "I want you to stay."

"I won't come between you and your brothers." Damn, a tear welled and slipped from the corner of her eye. Another popped up and followed the first.

"You aren't. We always argue like this." Sean glanced over her shoulder. "Don't we?"

Gabe grunted.

Tanner growled.

Sean's lips thinned. "Don't we?"

"Yeah." Gabe and Tanner answered as one.

"Ah, hell, Isabella. We're all smitten with you," Tanner admitted.

"I'm sorry. I shouldn't have let it go this far." She looked up into Sean's green eyes, so much like his brothers'. "Let go of me. I need to leave."

"No, you don't." Sean kissed the tear off her cheek. "Let us prove to you that we can play well together." He thumbed another tear from her chin. "Let us show you how good it can be with the three of us. We promise to make you happy."

His voice soothed over her like velvet, warming her in places that hadn't felt warm in a long time. Her logical self argued that no good could come of being with three men, while her heart disagreed, tilting her toward Sean's chest.

He gathered her in his arms and held her, brushing her wet hair back off her forehead. He pressed a kiss to the tip of her nose, then her lips. "Trust me," he whispered.

Her arms rose, circling his neck. She should have fought the yearning, slayed the desire and moved back into her lonely existence in her dinky apartment, counting her pennies until she could buy Sundance back from the Circle C. Even with the little over two thousand dollars she'd saved, she doubted it would be enough to convince Daniel to sell Sundance to her. Who was she kidding? Daniel was a bastard, willing to jack the price up just to piss her off.

Sean scooped her legs from beneath her and carried her back out into the pool, taking her to his brothers where he set her on her feet between the three of them.

One by one, they touched her, their hands roving over her skin. Gabe cupped a breast.

Tanner's cock nudged her from behind and Sean's dick bumped her in the front.

Heat flamed inside her belly, spreading like a wildfire out of control.

Gabe pinched her nipple, then his hand stilled. "We didn't bring protection."

"I'm on the Pill," she said.

"We're all clean, no STDs," Tanner offered.

"Then what are we waiting for?" Isabella grasped Sean's cock. "Remind me how much bigger you are than your brothers." She winked at Gabe.

"He's not." Tanner pressed his dick between her butt cheeks.

"Let her be the judge." Sean's smile lit the shadows beneath the overhanging trees as he lifted her, guiding her legs around his middle. He held her poised over his dick.

"Wait, let me prime her engine." Gabe slid his hand over her mound, his finger finding and gliding into her channel. "Oh, yeah. She's wet."

"Wet-wet, or creek-wet," Sean asked, his voice strained. "I don't know how much longer I can wait."

"He'll shoot his wad like a randy teen." Gabe jerked his head. "Let a real man show her how it's done."

"Guys." Isabella shook her head. "You can all show me in your own way." She eased herself down over Sean's shaft. "Ummm. That's right. You *are* big." Her breath caught as Sean filled her, stretching her tight channel. "What was that thing Gabe did last night?"

Gabe nodded to Tanner. "The lady likes a little anal sex. Can you manage?"

"Can I? Huh." Tanner's fingers dove beneath the water,

following the crease of her ass to her anus. He poked a finger in. "How's this?"

Isabella sucked in a short breath and blew it out. "Yes. More, please."

Gabe cupped her chin and turned her to face him. "Is this the way you want it? All three of us at once? Every time?"

The question caught her in the middle of a wave of passion. With Sean in her pussy, Tanner fingering her anus and Gabe cupping her breasts, Isabella had never felt more alive or desirable, capable of anything, especially orgasm. "Yes!"

"What if we don't want to share you?" Tanner asked from behind her, sending a second finger inside her.

Her breathing constricted, her thoughts wrapped around what they were doing to her body. "You're asking me now?"

"Yes," Tanner replied.

"If it's too much to ask—" She sucked in a breath and tried to focus, her channel contracting around Sean's thickness. "I'll understand." Her breath whooshed out and she sucked in another.

"What does that mean?" Gabe asked, his fingers tightening on her chin. "What will you do?"

Her brows rose, her eyes widening, a single tear slipping from the corner of one eye. "I'll leave you all alone. I won't drive a wedge between brothers." She stilled, forcing back the need for these men to fuck her hard and fast. "Is that what you want? Me to make a choice?" She shook her head.

"Good grief, Tanner, Gabe, leave it." Sean held Isabella's hips in his hands, his fingers squeezing her flesh. "She wants all of us. I, for one, am willing." He smiled down at Isabella. "She's a lot of woman to love."

Gabe nodded. "Don't make a decision now." He stroked her tit, tweaking the nipple, his hand sliding over her torso and downward to her swollen, throbbing nubbin. "Let us pleasure you. Forget what I said."

Given her current connection with Sean and Tanner, with Gabe strumming her clit, Isabella let the conversation slide to the back of her mind.

Sean pushed up inside her, his hands pressing her down over him at the same time. He settled into a rhythm, sliding in and out, increasing his speed until he rocked like a piston.

Tanner's probing continued matching Sean's pace, Gabe's fingers flicking at her clit.

"Oh, sweet heaven." Sean jerked to a halt, his jaw tightening, his head thrown back. "I want to stay here forever."

"You got that right." Tanner said, his fingers sliding into Isabella's anus.

With the two men inside her and one flicking the bundle of nerves, she thought the water around her would boil as hot as she was.

Tanner slipped free.

Sean thrust once more, then pulled out, his breath labored, his body rigid, his jaw tight. "Incredible. Absolutely incredible." When he had himself under control, he kissed her lips. "Now, your turn." He carried her to a rock ledge, setting her bottom on the cool stone.

"Let me." Tanner spread her legs, draping them over

his shoulders, and tongued her clit, flicking and teasing, sucking at the little nubbin.

Gabe climbed up beside and stroked her breasts, pinching the nipples between his thumbs.

Though her body soared, her heart hurt at the possibility of choosing between them or leaving them alone.

For now, she just wanted to love each one of them.

Isabella reached out and wrapped her hand around Gabe's cock. "I want you too." She tugged gently, lying back on the rock, urging him to straddle her.

Gabe placed a knee on either side of her head, spreading his legs wide enough to lower himself over her, then he dropped to all fours, his cock sliding into her mouth.

She grabbed his buttocks, her fingers sinking in, pulling him closer. Giving pleasure while receiving it sent Isabella bursting over the top. Tingles started in her fingers and toes and spread like lightning, shooting toward the center of her body. Her back arched and she cried out, the sound muffled by Gabe's shaft. She urged Gabe to pump faster as Tanner's tongue strokes sped, his fingers slipping in and out of her cunt.

Gabe tensed, his dick deep in her mouth.

Isabella quivered, another intense orgasm rocking her. She sucked hard on Gabe's cock, every nerve in her body strung as tight as a bowstring.

Gabe yanked free, his come shooting out over the rock beside her.

Yes. Isabella liked that he'd peaked in her mouth, that she could make him so crazy with lust he'd hit the big "O" while making love to her with his brothers present.

Before Isabella's waves of sensations waned, Tanner stood and slipped inside her slick, drenched channel.

He thrust deep, his hands curled around her thighs, his mouth set in a thin line as he pumped in and out.

Isabella lifted her legs, wrapping them around his waist, urging him to go faster, deeper and as hard as he could. She wanted him to fuck her like a jackhammer, again and again, his balls slapping against her buttocks.

He jerked free, breathing hard and grinning, his come jetting across her belly. "You're amazing, Isabella." He kissed her. "I'd have stayed a little longer, but without a condom...I just wanted to be extra safe."

She laughed out loud as she fell back to earth, her body going limp in the wake of the most satisfying sexual experience of her life.

Gabe, Tanner and Sean spread out on the rock ledge near her.

Life didn't get better than this. "I could live like this," she whispered.

"What did you say?" Gabe asked.

Isabella smiled. "I've never had a more beautiful day." Even as she said the words aloud, she knew it was all a dream. No woman had the right to claim three men. Ultimately, she'd have to make a choice.

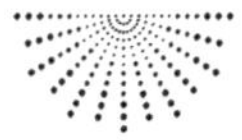

CHAPTER EIGHT

Gabe called a meeting of his brothers in the barn the next morning.

Tanner, Sean and Jesse lounged against the walls.

"Why are we having a meeting?" Jesse asked.

"You don't have to stay, if you don't want to. I know you need to get ready for the wedding. This conversation doesn't really have much to do with you, anyway."

"I do need to check on a few things before the wedding party arrives." Jesse straightened and glanced at his watch. "What does your little meeting have to do with?"

"Isabella," Gabe responded.

With a grin, Jesse settled back against a stall door. "Then I guess I'll hear you out. The details can wait. I have plenty of time."

Gabe shook his head. "You already have a fiancé."

"Yeah, but it's been fun watching you three fight over

one lady." He nodded toward his other brothers. "Go on. I'll just listen."

"I wanted you all to know I invited Isabella to use the barn and ride the horses any time she wants."

Sean clapped his hands together, grinning. "Great. I can't wait to see her again. When's she coming?"

"That's just it." Gabe's lips thinned. "She said she wouldn't come if we crowd her. She told me that she understands the need to decide between the three of us, and she doesn't want to be pressured."

Tanner frowned. "You mean we can't come around when she's here?"

"She didn't exactly say that, but she doesn't want us pushing her to decide."

"Okay, I'm good with that." Sean grinned. "When will she be here?"

"I know the answer to that one." Jesse crossed his arms, a smirk lifting one side of his mouth. "I invited her to the wedding."

Gabe, Tanner and Sean all shot looks at his brother.

"I get to sit with her," Sean said first.

"No." Jesse laughed. "You're in the wedding, moron."

"At the barbeque then."

Gabe shook his head. "Let her decide. Remember, no pressure."

Sean's happy face slid into a stern look. "And no arguing over her. You almost had her running last time we were…together."

"Look at the younger brother telling the older ones how to behave." Jesse clapped a hand on Sean's back. "Chalk one up for the youngsters. Now, we have a wedding to get through. Let's get going. I'm ready to start my honeymoon." Jesse strode from the barn, whistling the wedding march.

"He's too damned happy," Tanner growled.

"Cut him some slack." Gabe draped an arm around Tanner's shoulders. "He's getting married in a few hours."

"And we still don't have a girl." Tanner stepped away from Gabe's arm.

"We could if you two would get over yourselves," Sean muttered.

"Think about it, Sean. How would we walk down the aisle at our own wedding with one bride and three grooms?" Gabe shook his head. "For one, it would look really weird and secondly, it's illegal."

Sean raised his hands in the air. "Who said we had to marry?"

Gabe laughed. "Are you kidding? Dad is hell-bent on marrying all of us off. The man wants grandkids."

Tanner nodded. "Yeah. He'll want us to make it legal and all."

Sean's brows rose. "Look at who's talking grandkids and marriage." He chuckled. "Weren't you the one adamantly against our father pushing us into marrying?"

"Shut up," Tanner warned. "I can still kick your ass."

"You two get a grip." Gabe jerked his head toward the barn door. "Come on, we have a wedding to go to." And Isabella was coming to it.

Isabella grabbed Audrey's arm. "I can't do this."

"Do what? You're going to a wedding, not an inquisition." Audrey hooked Isabella's arm through hers. "You'll be fine. Those O'Brien brothers aren't going to make you do anything you don't want to do."

"Except decide which one I want."

Audrey came to an abrupt halt. "Just what *do* you want?"

Isabella rolled her eyes, throwing her hand in the air. "I don't know. I haven't been seeing them long enough to know anything."

"Bull crackers!" Audrey fisted her hand on her hips. "You've talked with them off and on for months at the Ugly Stick. And now you've made love to all of them if I got your vibes right."

Her cheeks heating, Isabella glanced around. "Shhh. Someone might hear you."

"And what?" Audrey grinned. "Some girl might get jealous? I know I'm a little green with envy. Three guys making love to me at once…feels pretty darned good, doesn't it?"

Isabella's brows rose. "You?"

Her boss winked. "I might be older than you, but not by much. And yes, I've had three men make love to me at once. It's pretty damned hot."

"But you're with Jackson now."

"Yeah." She smiled. "But that was an easy decision. I only ever wanted Jackson, not his two brothers. If I'd wanted all three, I wouldn't have settled for less. So why are you?"

"Gabe and Tanner aren't willing to share for the long-term."

"Then let them know it's all or nothing." Audrey continued forward, dragging Isabella with her. "Simple."

If only it was that simple.

Isabella took a seat in the back row with Audrey.

Jackson joined them, lowering his length into the chair beside Audrey.

As people filed in and settled, Isabella craned her neck to catch a glimpse of her three O'Brien brothers.

Good Lord, she was already calling them hers when no one had made any such commitment.

A man playing guitar accompanied a woman singing and the bridal party began the procession down the aisle, starting with the groomsmen leading the bridesmaids to the altar.

Gabe came first with Charli Sutton on his arm. Charli was a vision in pale, lemon yellow, the color complementing her long blonde hair.

A stab of jealousy wedged into Isabella's chest until Charli winked at Connor Mason, her fiancé. Charli was set on a fall wedding and Connor obviously couldn't wait.

Gabe winked at Isabella, making butterflies take wing in her belly.

Tanner marched down the aisle next, Libby Jones at his side, his face as serious as only Tanner could do and still look so incredibly handsome it made Isabella's heart flutter. As he passed her, he paused and handed her a single white rose.

Isabella's cheeks burned as she became the center of attention when in actuality she was a late invitee to the wedding. But how sweet of Tanner, the stoic, to pause long enough to hand her a flower.

Isabella almost laughed at Libby's Kiowa cowboys, Mark and Luke Gray Wolf, as they sat near the front, frowning fiercely until Tanner left Libby's side to take his position beside his brothers. Isabella thought how nice it would be to be loved that much by more than one man.

Her heart melted and her gaze followed Gabe and Tanner to the arched trellis where Jesse stood waiting for his bride.

Sean practically sauntered down the aisle, smiling as if it was his day and he was about to be married.

Molly O'Brien clung to Sean's arm, struggling to keep up in her high heels, giggling instead of cursing when she stumbled.

As Sean passed Isabella, he blew her a kiss.

Any time Isabella was around Sean, he made her smile. The man had a joy for life unrivaled by any of his brothers. Any woman would be lucky to have such an optimist for a husband.

Husband? Isabella rose as the organ player struck up Mendelssohn's *Wedding March*, and Ellie Lang and her father started down the aisle.

Isabella could barely take her gaze off the beautiful bride.

Ellie wore a long white strapless gown with a sweetheart neckline, and embroidered lace with hand-sewn beadwork overlaying a satin lining. The skirt flared out below the hips, ending in a short cathedral train. As Ellie stepped forward, the tips of her white cowboy boots peeked from beneath the hemline. Her gaze centered on Jesse O'Brien.

The O'Brien men stood tall and straight, all dressed in

black tuxedos and crisp white cotton shirts. Every one of them dark-haired, green-eyed and gorgeous.

A lump lodged in Isabella's throat as Ellie stepped up to the Justice of the Peace.

The ceremony went off without a hitch, the bride and groom exchanging their vows, their happiness shining from their faces. The JP pronounced them husband and wife and a cheer went up, Texas-style. Loud and rowdy.

Isabella wiped away a tear, studying Gabe, Tanner and Sean as they congratulated their brother and new sister-in-law.

As one, the three turned her direction.

Her stomach flip-flopped, heat rising in her cheeks. How could she choose between them? Each had a quality she utterly adored. Together, they made her feel complete. If she chose only one and they actually married, she'd be a part of the family, constantly in contact with the other two. Would the two she didn't select harbor resentment for the brother who'd won?

Could Isabella bear to see them move on, find other women and start a family apart from her? It would only be fair, but she couldn't do it. These men were too special. Forced to choose, she knew she couldn't.

The reception and dance following the wedding cere-mony lasted long after sunset. Isabella had ridden with Audrey, who showed no sign of leaving early.

Jackson had her out on the dance floor, spinning her around in her bright red cowboy boots.

Isabella retreated to Audrey's truck where she'd stashed a set of clothes on the off chance she'd find a chance to get away.

Gabe had given her carte blanche to ride whenever she felt like it. Right then, she felt like riding. Anything to get away from the happiness emanating from the newly married couple.

Isabella changed in the truck and jogged down the rise to the barn. The gray mare she'd ridden the day before pawed at her stall door, tossing her head.

"How would you like to go riding in the moonlight, Stormy?" Isabella called out softly.

The horse whickered, her nostrils flaring.

Isabella led the horse out, slipped the bit in her mouth, and slid the straps over her ears, buckling them in place. Preferring to ride bareback, Isabella passed the tack room without going inside as she led the mare out into the night air.

Moonlight shone down, giving the landscape a deep blue glow.

Isabella opened the gate to the pasture, led the horse through and closed it behind her. Only a few steps away from freedom from the crowd, the O'Brien men and the conclusion she'd come to.

Her eyes flooding with tears, Isabella grabbed a handful of Stormy's mane and she swung up on her back. Then she reined the horse around and nudged her gently into a gallop, sending her away from the lights, music and men she'd come to adore.

GABE JOINED Sean at the edge of the dance floor constructed especially for the wedding party. The lights, the music, the food had all been perfect except... "Have you seen Isabella?"

Sean frowned. "I was just about to ask you the same."

"Where's Isabella?" Tanner joined them.

Gabe shrugged. "Neither one of us have seen her."

"Didn't she come with Audrey?" Tanner scanned the crowded dance floor.

Audrey and Jackson chose that time to break away from the other dancers.

Gabe went after her. "Audrey, wait up."

"Hi, Gabe." Audrey's face was flushed a bright pink, a thin film of perspiration making her glow. "Whatcha need?"

"Did Isabella leave?"

Audrey shook her head. "I don't know how, unless she caught a ride home with someone else."

"Have you seen her since the ceremony?"

"Last I saw her, she was heading for my truck, saying something about changing into something more comfortable. All she brought was jeans and her old cowboy boots."

As soon as Audrey mentioned boots, Gabe knew.

He rejoined his brothers. "I think she's gone riding. Come on."

"At night?"

"She likes riding bareback in the moonlight," Gabe said.

"Hot damn. I knew she was a woman after my own heart." Sean took off at a jog, passing his brothers as they headed for the barn.

Tanner ground to a halt, slamming an arm into Gabe. "Wait a minute. We can't go like this."

Sean skidded to a halt and glanced down at his tuxedo. "Damn. You're right." He performed an about-face and raced for the house.

Gabe was a length ahead of him, Tanner running neck and neck.

They all emerged from the house two minutes later in jeans and boots, shirts slung over their shoulders.

When they reached the barn, Gabe went straight for Stormy's stall.

Empty.

"She could be anywhere by now." Gabe ran a hand through his hair.

"We have to find her. What if she falls?" Tanner led his mare out of a stall. "What if Stormy steps in an armadillo hole and throws Isabella?"

"She's a better rider than all three of us. I doubt any of that will happen." At least Gabe hoped nothing happened to her.

Sean turned from the saddle racks. "She didn't take a saddle."

Tanner's lips thinned. "What if the horse gets spooked?" He slipped the bridle over his mare's head and buckled it in place. Without waiting to saddle up, he headed for the door.

Sean's brows rose. "No saddle?"

"No time." Tanner exited, swinging up on the horse's back. "She can't be too far ahead."

"Assuming you know which way she went." Sean led his gelding outside and to the pasture gate, unlatching, then opening it.

"Not knowing the terrain very well, I'll bet she lets the

horse decide." Gabe mounted his stallion bareback and rode through.

Sean laughed. "Stormy will go for the pool. She always does."

Gabe dug his heels into the stallion's flanks.

Drago leapt forward into a gallop.

Sean and Tanner followed.

Although cooler than the daytime heat, the night remained warm and balmy, the heat of the day's sunlight absorbed in the earth.

All along the way, Gabe kept an eye out for any signs of Isabella or Stormy.

Not until they reached the crest of the hill overlooking the creek below did he see the horse or rider.

As soon as he topped the hill, he spotted Isabella, standing in the moonlight beside the horse, her body a blue-tinged silhouette against the black backdrop of the trees.

His brothers reined in beside him.

"What's she doing?" Sean asked.

Isabella's arms rose above her head and she tossed something to the side.

Gabe's heartbeat galloped, his groin tightening. "Looks like she's stripping."

Tanner whistled. "Damn, she's beautiful in the moonlight."

Although his first inclination was to race down the hill and join her, Gabe hesitated. As did his brothers.

"Would it be pressuring her if we joined her now?" Tanner asked, for once tentative, so unlike his normal brusque, confident self.

Gabe's chest squeezed. "Maybe."

"What if we don't mention her decision?" Sean's horse danced to the side, eager to descend to the creek. "We could tell her the horses were thirsty."

Gabe snorted. "Like she'd believe it."

"I think it's worth trying." Tanner hadn't taken his gaze off Isabella since arriving at the top of the hill.

"How do you feel now about sharing her between the three of us?" Gabe asked Tanner.

Tanner sucked in a breath and let it out slowly. "I'd rather have her between us than not at all. If we make her choose, two, if not all of us, will lose out."

"I've been thinking about that too." Gabe's gaze returned to Isabella.

She bent to remove her boots, then her jeans. The moonlight reflected off her pale skin, accentuating every curve.

"I'd rather have her love all of us than choose between us and be hurt by it." Gabe's gut knotted. "The thought of seeing her all the time would kill me, knowing I couldn't hold her."

"Same here," Tanner agreed.

"About time you boneheads came to your senses." Sean nodded toward Isabella. "So do we go down or not?"

"We go." Gabe nudged his horse, sending it over the crest and down the incline toward the creek.

In the distance, Isabella waded into the water, sending ripples across its glassy surface.

Riding bareback, Gabe had kept his horse at a walk or a gallop. Trotting was too hard on his balls. Now, when he wanted speed, he knew it would be no good to go racing toward the creek, only frightening Isabella or her horse. Instead the three brothers approached at a sedate pace.

As they neared, Isabella dove beneath the surface.

Gabe reined in beside Stormy and slid off Drago's back. He held his breath, waiting for Isabella to come up. After a moment or two, he stepped forward.

Isabella emerged, rising slowing until she stood in water waist-deep, her back to the men.

Had she not heard them riding down the hill?

Gathering his breath, Gabe prepared to clear his throat to get her attention.

"Are you just going to stand there or are you coming in?" She gave them a wicked glance over her shoulder and dove under.

Gabe ripped his shirt off his back, shucked his boots and jeans and dove in.

Two splashes reverberated through the water as he broke through the surface.

Isabella floated on her back, her nipples rising above the water, glistening in the moonlight.

All three men cleaved the water, getting to her in seconds.

"Why did you leave the party?" Sean asked. "Not that I'm complaining. The view here is much better."

"Being surrounded by all that happiness made me sad." She let her feet drop to the creek bottom and she reached out to touch Sean's cheek. "I needed time to think."

"Are we intruding?" Gabe asked. "I promised we wouldn't pressure you."

"No pressure. Please stay." With her other hand, she

trailed her fingers down Gabe's chest, setting his body on fire. "I think, deep down, I wanted y'all to follow me."

"All of us?" Tanner closed in on her other side, his expression dark, a muscle ticking in his jaw.

She smiled. "Dear Tanner. You are always so serious." She cupped his chin and kissed him. "Yes. All of you."

Tanner closed his eyes, letting go of the breath he'd obviously been holding. "Thank God."

Isabella pulled in a deep breath and let it out slowly. "I've made my decision."

A knot settled in Gabe's gut. Even before she spoke, he knew he wasn't going to like what she had to say.

"I can't be with you three. Tonight will be the last night we can be together."

"No." Sean reached for her, pulling her into his arms. "We've decided. We're willing to love you on your own terms. If that means sharing, we're in."

Isabella glanced from Gabe to Tanner. "All of you?"

Gabe nodded. "Absolutely."

"Damn right." Tanner lifted her hand and kissed her knuckles. "We want you no matter what."

She shook her head. "Much as I love you all, I can't do that to you. You deserve to be happy like Jesse. One woman each. It's selfish of me to want the love of all three of you."

"We don't care." Gabe smoothed a hand down her cheek, his chest tightening at her mention of love. "We want you any way we can have you. I'd rather share you with my brothers than lose you altogether."

She shook her head. "Don't you see? You're settling for something you really don't want."

"I love you, Isabella," Tanner spoke softly, but his words carried across the shadows. "I love what you do to me when you're with me and my brothers. You're the woman for us."

"We all love you," Sean added.

"Then show me, because it will be our last time." A tear slipped down Isabella's cheek and fell into the pool.

Gabe dragged her into his arms and kissed her, his tongue pushing past her teeth, delving deep, twining with hers. He wanted to hold her until she changed her mind, until she knew how much they loved her and would do anything for her. Soon, he broke off and handed her to Tanner.

Tanner lifted her, settling her legs around his waist. He kissed her, thrusting into her at the same time.

Sean wrapped his arms around her from behind, burying his face in her neck. "Please, Isabella, don't leave us."

"Shhh," she said, her head falling back, her eyes closed. "No words, just action."

In silence, Gabe and his brothers showed her just how much they'd come to care for her.

Tanner drove into her, drawing out their lovemaking until tears spilled from her eyes. When he'd climaxed, he lifted her off and passed her to Gabe.

Gabe floated her on her back, while Sean draped her legs over his shoulders and tongued her clit.

She cried out, her hand reaching behind her to capture Gabe's shoulders, her fingers digging in as her body arched out of the water.

Sean's relentless assault on Isabella's clit yielded a long, drawn-out sigh when she finally relaxed.

Gabe wished he'd been the one to bring her there, but he didn't begrudge his brother the pleasure of making their woman come. All of them pleasuring her made him even more excited, more determined to make her a permanent part of their lives.

"You all are amazing." She slipped her legs from Sean's shoulders and let her feet drift to the bottom. She turned to Gabe. "Can we go ashore?"

"Yes, ma'am." He lifted her in his arms and carried her to the huge rock they'd shared the day before. Laying her down, he stretched out beside her.

"How can I have all of you at once?" she whispered.

Gabe's cock twitched, his gut tightening, his body on fire, ready to take her. "Let us show you."

ISABELLA'S INSIDES shook with the intensity of her feelings for the men and what they were doing to her.

Gabe rolled her over onto her stomach and pulled her up to her hands and knees.

Tanner laid on his back and scooted beneath Isabella, positioning his head beneath her pussy, his cock below her mouth.

Sean parted Tanner's legs and dropped to his knees in front of Isabella.

Gabe knelt behind Isabella, his hands on her hips. "Will this do?"

She chuckled. "Oh, yes, it will." Then she gripped Sean's cock in her hand and guided it into her mouth, licking the tip, tapping the tiny hole oozing with pre-come.

Tanner flicked her clit with his work-roughened fingers, setting her on the path to the stars for the second time that night. If she didn't know better, she could become a nymphomaniac with these cowboys. They knew exactly how to make her body sing.

Gabe nudged her entrance with the tip of his engorged cock, pressing into her in a slow, easy glide.

Her hand tightened on Sean's cock as she leaned back, taking more of Gabe into her. "Harder," she begged. "Fuck me like it was your last time." As Gabe complied, Isabella sucked Sean's dick into her mouth.

With Gabe fucking her cunt, Tanner flicking her clit and Sean's cock filling her mouth, her senses swirled, her body throbbed and her heart beat so fast she couldn't breathe.

Sensations built, the electricity between the three of them exploding in a firestorm of lust and need.

Sean stilled, his muscles tensed, his eyes squeezed shut with the effort of controlling his release.

Isabella shot over the edge into her own orgasm. She grasped Sean's balls and squeezed, pulling her mouth away from his shaft to gasp for air, giving him the chance to come.

As soon as Sean released, he scooted back.

Isabella grasped Tanner's jutting cock and lowered herself to take him into her mouth, twirling her tongue around his big length.

His heels dug into the ground and he raised his hips, pumping deeper into her mouth. When Tanner came,

Isabella's head rose and she held her breath as the tingling started all over again, racing across her body like electrical shocks, racing toward her core.

Gabe grasped her hips in his big, coarse hands and thrust in once more, burying himself deep inside her as she rode the wave, his cock pulsing against her channel.

When she returned to earth, she rolled off Tanner and lay on her back, staring up at the stars between the gaps in the branches above, pleasantly exhausted. "I've never felt this complete."

"Me either," Gabe echoed.

Sean sighed. "I think I died and went to heaven."

"If this is heaven, Isabella is an angel," Tanner whispered, gathering her into his arms, spooning her from behind.

Gabe lay in front of her, his hands stroking her breasts, her belly, her mound.

If she died right then, she'd die the happiest and most fulfilled she'd ever been. But she was very much alive and it was time to go. Her throat closed off as tears filled her eyes again.

"We should be getting back," she choked out. "The horses need rest."

"The horses can wait." Tanner's arm tightened around her middle.

"No, really, I need to go. Audrey will be looking for me."

"We'll take you home."

"No, I'll ride with Audrey." She pushed to her feet and located her clothes, dragging them over her damp skin.

The men rose and joined her, pulling on jeans and boots, skipping their shirts.

Isabella grabbed Stormy's mane, swung up onto her back, nudged her into a gentle gallop, and headed for the barn.

Before she'd topped the hill, Gabe rode up on one side, Sean on the other, Tanner beside Sean.

They rode back to the ranch buildings in silence and dismounted.

Isabella slid off her horse and led Stormy toward the barn.

"We'll take care of Stormy," Sean offered.

Brushing away ready tears, Isabella nodded. "Thanks." She stood on her toes and kissed Sean and moved back before he could wrap his arms around her.

More tears spilled down her cheeks as she dragged Tanner's face down for a kiss.

Finally, she stood in front of Gabe.

He didn't lean toward her, his eyes glistening in the light from the party. "Don't go."

She shook her head, a sob rising up in her chest. "I have to. Now, kiss me goodbye."

He shook his head. "Not goodbye." Gabe crushed her in his arms, his mouth slanting over hers as he bent her over his arm. When he set her back on her feet, he sighed. "We're not over."

Unable to argue, Isabella turned and ran.

CHAPTER NINE

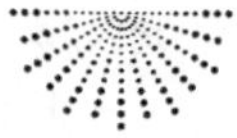

Tanner stormed into the Ugly Stick Saloon as soon as it opened the next afternoon. When he spotted Audrey sweeping the floor near the bar, he cornered her. "Where's Isabella?"

After glancing up briefly, Audrey continued her work. "She's not here. She quit."

"Then where the hell is she?" Tanner's heart thundered against his ribs. "She wasn't at her apartment."

Sean came up from behind and placed his foot in front of Audrey's broom. "Look, Audrey, we have to find her."

Audrey leaned against the broom handle, her lips quirking upward. "Well, she's not here."

Gabe's eyes narrowed. "But you know where she is, don't you?"

Her mouth twitched. "Yeah, but she swore me to secrecy."

Tanner slammed his palm on the bar. "Damn it, Audrey. You have to tell us."

Audrey fisted her hands on her hips. "I keep my promises. Besides, what are your intentions toward my Isabella?"

"We love her. We want to marry her," Tanner answered without a hint of hesitation.

Audrey snorted. "Now, all three of you can't marry her. Bigamy isn't legal in Texas."

"Who marries her doesn't matter. We all love her and we want her to be with us always."

"Your father was here this morning asking about Isabella. He likes her a lot and thinks one of you should marry her. I agree. A woman needs stability and a place to call home. So who will it be?"

"Me!" All three of them spoke at once.

"We're back to the problem of legality. Why don't you draw straws?" Audrey flipped the broom over and yanked out three straws of equal length, breaking one in half. She held out her hand, demonstrating the differences in length. "Okay, who will be the lucky fella?"

Tanner drew in a breath and let it out like a bull in the fighting ring. "This is ridiculous. You can't decide who a woman is going to marry by drawing straws."

"Well, if she won't choose, y'all have to." Audrey hid her hands behind her back.

"If choosing is all that's holding Isabella back from committing to us, I say let's draw." Sean reached out a hand. "Let me have one.

"You all need to choose at once. It wouldn't be fair otherwise." Audrey stared from Gabe to Tanner. "Are you in or not?"

Frustration threatened to burn a hole in Tanner's gut.

"You're crazy."

"I'm in." Gabe reached out.

Not to be left out, Tanner held out his hand as well. "As long as we all agree, it's only for legalities."

"Agreed," Sean said.

Gabe nodded. "Agreed."

"Now that you're all in agreement…draw." Audrey held out her hand, her fingers wrapped around the three straws that appeared to be roughly the same length.

The men pulled the one closest to them.

Tanner's heart sank when he drew a long straw. He wanted to be the one who married Isabella. She was perfect in every way.

Sean's mouth sank into a frown when he compared his straw to Tanner's.

Gabe's face split into a grin. "I win!"

"Remember, it's only for legal purposes," Tanner reminded him.

"Seems kind of fair anyway, Gabe being the oldest," Sean conceded. "Besides, now he has the task of convincing Isabella to marry him with the two of us thrown into the bargain." He slapped Gabe on the back. "Good luck, old man."

"We *all* have to convince her." Tanner clenched his fists, his jaw tightening. "We have to present a unified front or she won't go for it. She has to know she's getting all three of us. And we have to believe it in order to sell it to her." He stuck out his hand like one of the Three Musketeers. "Are we all in this together?"

Sean slapped his hand over Tanner's. "You bet."

Gabe laid his over the top. "I'm in."

Audrey sighed. "Well then, now all you have to do is find her."

Tanner glared at the bar owner. "You said you knew where."

"I do, but I said I wouldn't tell you."

"Does she have a big lead on us?" Sean asked.

"I told her I wouldn't tell y'all where, but she didn't say anything about when." Audrey smiled. "She left an hour ago."

Gabe snorted. "Are we going to play charades to get the answer?"

Audrey shrugged. "Sorry, boys, but a promise is a promise."

Tanner wanted to reach out and wring Audrey's neck. Instead he asked, "Within a fifty-mile radius?"

Audrey nodded. "I'll give you a hint. She's going to visit something she loves."

Sean scratched his head. "I didn't think she had any family left."

"Something?" Tanner closed his eyes and thought, trying to push the feeling that they were wasting time to the back of his mind. "Human, object or animal?"

"Definitely animal." Audrey grinned.

"Horses." Gabe's eyes shone. "Is she going after horses?"

Audrey's smile broadened. "Not plural."

"Where would she go after a horse?" Tanner wanted to shake Audrey. He hated guessing games.

"An auction?" Sean asked.

Audrey shook her head.

"A race track?" Gabe suggested.

She shook her head again.

"A ranch?"

"Bingo." Audrey's eyes lit.

"Good grief." Tanner flung his hands in the air. "There must be a hundred ranches in a fifty-mile radius."

"Then we better get to guessing." Sean nudged Tanner in the side. "We don't have all day."

"If you were to ask me where Isabella worked before she came to the Ugly Stick Saloon, I could answer that."

Tanner blurted, "Where did Isabella work before here?"

Audrey propped her hands on her hips. "The Circle C."

"The Circle C Ranch?" Gabe questioned. "As in the big racehorse ranch on the other side of Hole in the Wall?"

"That's where she used to work." Audrey laughed. "There, I didn't spill the beans on where she went. I only told you where she worked." She frowned. "What are you waiting for?"

Tanner beat the other two to the exit, slamming through and running toward the truck. He slid into the driver's seat and took the wheel, holding out his hand to Gabe. "Give me the keys."

"I'll drive." Gabe stood in the door, keeping Tanner from closing it.

"Give me the goddamn keys." Tanner refused to budge. "We need to find Isabella. We can't lose her."

Gabe tossed him the keys and scrambled into the back seat of the crew cab. "Go!"

Tanner broke every speed limit between the Ugly Stick Saloon and the Circle C Ranch.

"I'LL BET the Circle C is the ranch Isabella got fired from." Gabe sat in the back seat hanging onto the oh-shit handle, praying they'd arrive in one piece. "She ever tell you why that happened?"

Tanner and Sean shook their heads.

"The owner's son put the moves on her. When she didn't satisfy him, he fired her."

Sean slammed a fist on the armrest. "Bastard."

Tanner growled. "She's not going back to work for them."

"Let's hope not," Gabe said.

"No hope about it." Tanner's jaw tightened. "She's *not* going back to work for the Circle C."

"Why else would she return to the ranch she was fired from?" Sean asked.

"I'm not sure," Gabe replied. "But in her apartment she had a picture of a horse. Maybe she's going back to get the horse." He hoped like hell Isabella wasn't going back to the coward who fired her. Gabe would pound the punk into the dirt before he let Isabella go back to that lowlife.

Tanner spun sideways when he took the turn onto the road leading up to the Circle C Ranch. They passed under a fancy arched gate with an iron horse in the design.

The drive wound through green pastures dotted with long-legged thoroughbreds prancing with their heads held high.

Gabe appreciated fine horseflesh, and the animals on the Circle C had good confirmation and were groomed beautifully. He couldn't fault the animals, even if the owners didn't have a lick of sense.

As Tanner pulled into the stable yard, Gabe's stomach

plummeted.

"I don't see her truck," Sean stated the obvious.

A well-dressed young man and older woman standing beside a corral turned as the brothers' truck came to a halt.

Tanner shifted into park. "What do you want to do?"

Heat spiked in Gabe's chest as he realized who the two people were. "I want to talk to the owners."

He jumped down out of the truck and strode toward the pair, coaching himself to keep his cool.

The older woman smiled graciously. "I'm Margaret Cooksey and this is my son, Daniel. Can we help you?"

Gabe held out his hand to the woman and shook her hand. "I'm Gabe O'Brien, these are my brothers, Tanner and Sean." He pointedly dropped his hand without offering it to the woman's son. He was too afraid he'd deck the guy.

Tanner and Sean moved up on either side of him.

His brothers' presence gave Gabe the incentive to continue without causing a scene. "We were looking for Isabella Severs. Has she been by here?"

The young man frowned. "Why? What do you want with her?"

Digging deep, Gabe forced a smile to his face when he'd rather plant his knuckles in the young man's sneering countenance. "We wanted to hire her to work on our ranch."

Neither Tanner nor Sean flinched at Gabe's lie. God, he loved his brothers.

The old woman smiled. "Izzy was here a few minutes ago. You just missed her."

"Why would you want to hire Izzy?" the young man asked.

"Daniel, where's your manners?" Mrs. Cooksey admonished. "Izzy is wonderful with horses and a really hard little worker. I miss having her around."

"As her future employer, could you tell me why Isabella left?" Gabe knew the answer, but wanted to hear what Daniel and his mother would say was the reason.

Daniel's eyes narrowed. "It's none of your business."

"Don't mind my son, he can be so brusque." Margaret's brows furrowed. "I don't know why she quit. One day she was just fine, working with the horses and seemingly happy. The next day she left. I was stunned she didn't even stop by the house to say goodbye." She glanced up at Gabe. "Not a very good recommendation, I'm sorry to say."

"Maybe she had good reason to leave." Gabe glanced at Daniel.

"Yes, but I couldn't believe she'd leave Sundance," Margaret offered. "She was very attached to him."

Tanner frowned. "Sundance?"

"The thoroughbred she sold to us when her father died. She came to work for us the day we bought him."

"What happened to Sundance?" Sean asked.

Margaret laughed. "That's the funny thing—"

"That's enough." Daniel stepped between his mother and Gabe. "If you don't have business with the Circle C, I suggest you leave. You're trespassing on private property."

"I might just have business with you…" Gabe stood toe-to-toe with the owner's son, " …if you can tell me where this horse Sundance can be found."

"What does it matter?" Daniel shrugged. "Like Izzy, he's not here."

"Don't be so rude." Margaret stepped to the side of her son. "Daniel decided that since Sundance hadn't placed in his last two races, he should be sold. I wanted to give him another chance. The poor dear had been acting strange since Izzy left. Those two were inseparable. Why, shoot, she raised him since he was a colt." She smiled sadly. "But that's neither here nor there. He went to the auction in Dallas two days ago. Which is quite a shame considering Izzy just offered us as much as Sundance brought, so we could have saved time and money getting him there."

"Mother," Daniel said through gritted teeth, "you talk too much."

"I supposed I do sometimes." Her smile broadened. "Would you boys like to come up to the ranch house for some iced tea? I'm headed that way now."

Gabe shook his head. "Sorry, ma'am, we can't stay. We have work to do." *And Isabella to find.* "Thank you for your time."

He waited until the woman climbed into a golf cart and drove away before he faced Daniel.

As soon as his mother was out of earshot, Daniel glared at Gabe and his brothers. "I suggest you boys leave before I call the sheriff and have you all arrested for trespassing."

"Now that you can't hide behind your mother, I want to set the record straight." Gabe stepped up to Daniel. "Isabella is a beautiful, sexy woman, filled with warmth and love…" He paused and stared hard into Daniel's eyes. "And more than capable of being satisfied by the right men. If she wasn't able to come for you, it wasn't because of her." Gabe stepped back, afraid he'd hit the man if he didn't.

Sean came forward and spit on the man's boots. "Obviously you weren't man enough for her." Sean spun away.

"What the hell did that whore tell you? She's nothing but a lying bitch."

Tanner shook his head. "You shoulda kept your mouth shut."

Before Gabe could grab him, Tanner swung hard, his fist connecting with Daniel's nose.

The man dropped to his knees. "I'll sue you for this," he blubbered, clutching at his face.

"Yeah, you do that." Gabe kicked dust in the coward's face. "While you're at it, we'll have the sheriff come out and haul your ass to jail for sexual harassment of one of your employees." He spun on his boot heels and headed for the truck, holding out his hand for the keys.

Tanner handed them over, no argument.

Once all three men were inside the truck and on their way back down the drive leaving the Circle C Ranch, Gabe let it out. "That son of a bitch." Gabe smacked his hand on the steering wheel. "You know what we have to do, don't you?"

"Go back and finish pounding some manners into that little weasel." Sean raised his fists.

Tanner rubbed his bloody knuckles. "We need to find Isabella."

"No to the pounding. The man's not worth any more of our time. Yes to finding Isabella, but not yet." Gabe pulled out onto the highway and pressed the accelerator to the floor, sending the truck rocketing toward the Rockin' O Ranch. "First, we have to find that horse."

"HONEY, you can't lie in bed for the rest of your life." Audrey sat on the edge of the mattress, stroking Isabella's hair away from her face.

Isabella had blown through a full box of tissues in twenty-four hours. "Why should I bother? That bastard sold my horse and had the nerve to laugh in my face."

"I hope you kicked him in the nuts."

"No, I told him he was the loser." Isabella's lips twitched in a brief smile. "You should have seen the look on his face when I told him I'd been having sex with three men and all of them had given me an orgasm."

"I'd have paid money to see that." Audrey grinned. "That's the Isabella I know and love."

"But it's no use. My affair with the O'Briens is over." Isabella flopped onto her back. "And now that Sundance is gone, I have nothing left to live for."

Audrey snorted. "Don't be so melodramatic. You have a lot to live for."

"Name one thing."

Audrey stared around the room. "You have your health…"

"That doesn't count." Isabella draped an arm over her face. "I lost Sundance, the only friend I had."

Audrey crossed her arms, a frown wrinkling her pretty brow. "What does that make me?"

"Oh, Audrey, you're such a good friend." Isabella gave

her a weak smile, and more tears welled in her eyes, spilling down her cheeks. "And I don't deserve you."

"You're right. You don't. Not the way you're acting now."

"See? I'm a failure."

Audrey rolled her eyes. "You have a job, should you decide to come to work."

"I told you," Isabella pulled a pillow over her face, "I have to leave town," she said, her voice muffled.

"You're running away, Isabella." Audrey yanked the pillow off her face. "That's no way to handle your troubles."

"It's the only way. I can't stay."

"Why?"

"I just can't." Isabella rolled away from her friend's penetrating stare.

"Because you love three men?"

"That sounds so wrong," Isabella wailed.

"If it's how you feel, how wrong can it be?" Audrey pressed her shoulder, forcing Isabella to lie on her back. "Look at me."

"No. You can't fix this."

"There's nothing to fix, silly." Her friend smiled down at her. "Just let them love you."

"But their father wants them to marry. He told me so."

"So, marry one of them, but love all three."

"I can't."

"Why?"

"None of them has asked. And I'm not sure it'll work. What if they fight? What if they get jealous of one another? I don't want to break up their family. Please. Go away and let me wallow."

"No. You're getting up and coming to work with me. I'm short some girls. I need your help."

"I don't work for you anymore."

Audrey planted her hands on her hips. "Who took you in when you were flat broke?"

Guilt gnawed at Isabella's gut. "You did."

"And you'd let me down after all I did for you?" Audrey glared at Isabella and turned her back. "Some friend."

"Don't ask me to do this…I…I…just can't." Audrey had done a lot for her. More than Isabella could ever repay.

"Now's the time when you should be saying 'I'm sorry, Audrey. Of course I'll come to work for you.'" Audrey glanced over her shoulder, her brows raised, utterly relentless.

Isabella sighed. "You're right. I'm sorry. I don't know what came over me. You've been nothing but kind to me and I've been a complete heel."

"You don't have to grovel that low, but that'll do for a start." Audrey spun, grabbed the edge of the sheet and yanked it back. "Now, get out of bed and get dressed. We open in one hour."

Isabella rolled over the edge onto her feet, groaning, her eyes filling with tears yet again. "How will I be able to serve if I can't see through my tears?" She ran for the bathroom and tore off several sheets of toilet paper and blew into them.

"You'll manage. You'll see." Audrey smiled. "I think you'll feel much better once you get to the Ugly Stick Saloon."

"I don't have your confidence."

Audrey crossed both arms. "Have I ever given you bad advice?"

Isabella thought through all the time she'd spent with Audrey. "The time you recommended the hot wings. I thought I'd eaten battery acid. The sauce was hot enough to strip paint."

"Okay, other than the hot wings?" Audrey waited.

"No."

"Exactly." Audrey threw a bright turquoise blouse at Isabella. "Jump in the shower, then put that on. The better you look, the better you'll feel."

"Whatever." Isabella stepped into the bathroom, switched on the shower and stripped out of her T-shirt and panties. She didn't feel like showering or getting dressed, but if she didn't, Audrey would do it for her.

The shower revived her a little, washing away the ravages of her tears. When she'd dried off, she slid her arms into the blouse and tied a knot at her waist, exposing her midriff, then walked out into her bedroom.

"Better." Audrey nodded. "If you show up like that, I guarantee you'll get all the tips for the night. I'd tip you myself."

Isabella glared at Audrey. "I'm not working in nothing but a shirt." She reached into her panty drawer and pulled out a black lace thong.

"Still, you're pretty damned hot in that. Stirs my juices, and I'm completely happy with Jackson. Hmm. I wonder if he'd go for a threesome with another girl…"

Isabella straightened, her troubles melting away at the heat in Audrey's gaze. Then Isabella shook her head.

"Sorry, I've never gone there with a woman, and with three men to choose from, I'm confused enough."

The beautiful blonde owner of the Ugly Stick Saloon shrugged. "Let us know if you change your mind. Jackson's pretty flexible…when I want him to be." Audrey rescued a pair of cutoffs from the floor. "In the meantime, wear these if you're not up to a little exhibition."

When Isabella had on clothes and her cowboy boots, Audrey hooked her arm and dragged her toward the door.

"What's your hurry?" Isabella stalled. "I thought Libby was opening the bar tonight?"

"We have a surprise special event I can't be late for."

Isabella groaned. "What event? I don't recall anything on the schedule." She wasn't up to a huge crowd. Hell, she wasn't up to anything at that moment.

"It wouldn't be a surprise if I told you, now would it?"

Isabella dug her boot heels into the carpet. "You're not planning anything around me, are you?"

Audrey's brows wrinkled. "Not everything revolves around you, dear."

She let Audrey drag her out the door and into her bright red pickup. "I can drive myself."

"I don't trust you to get there."

"Yet you expect me to trust you? That's just wrong in so many ways."

Audrey crooked her thumb toward her truck. "Get in. I promise you'll feel better once you're at the Ugly Stick."

Isabella climbed into the cab and leaned her head against the cool window. "I have to pack."

"One day at a time, dear."

"I have to give notice to my landlord."

"Focus, Isabella. You have to work tonight."

Dusk settled into night as, one by one, the stars twinkled to life in the huge Texas sky.

Why did the stars have to shine? They only reminded Isabella of the wedding night when she'd gone skinny-dipping in the creek with Gabe, Sean and Tanner. Her heart squeezed so tightly her chest hurt. She had to remind herself that she was doing the right thing. The O'Brien men deserved to find the loves of their lives. Each one settling down with a wife, having children and gracing their father with all the grandchildren he could manage. The way it *should* be.

Trucks and cars lined the parking lot at the Ugly Stick Saloon.

Isabella raised her head, her feet already hurting with the thought of all the drinks she'd be serving to keep up with the crowd if she was one of the only waitresses there. "Wow, you weren't kidding you needed help."

"See? I wouldn't have dragged you out of your bed if it wasn't important."

"You can count on me." Isabella squared her shoulders, preparing for a rough night. "For tonight. After that, I really have to find a job in another town. I can't be here and watch them fall in love with someone else."

"Worry about that tomorrow, honey." Audrey parked the truck out front.

"Why aren't you parking in the rear?"

"Uh, I had some work done on the asphalt back there. We have to let it dry before we can drive on it." She yanked the keys from the ignition and jumped down. "Come on, Libby's probably dying in there."

Isabella eased down out of the truck, her heart breaking all over again, a fresh wash of tears welling. She'd first met the O'Brien man at the Ugly Stick. She'd made love to them on the dance floor a little more than a week ago. Her feet drifted to a stop.

"Oh no, you're not backing out on me now. You have to go inside." Audrey hooked Isabella's arm and dragged her across the pavement to the entrance.

"I can't."

"You can. Trust me." Audrey hugged her close. "I love you, girl. You can do this." Then she turned her to face the door, swung it inward and pushed Isabella through.

"She's here!" someone shouted.

Isabella blinked, trying to focus on the crowd in the barroom. Something big stood in the center of the dance floor. Bigger than a man and shaped like a…

"Is that a horse?" Isabella whispered.

Audrey leaned close to her ear. "Not just a horse. Go on. See for yourself."

Isabella's heart skipped several beats and then raced ahead.

The horse tossed his head and whickered as if sensing her presence.

"Sundance?" Isabella stumbled forward, tears filling her eyes. "Is that you, boy?"

The crowded bar was surprisingly quiet, every cowboy and cowgirl in the place aware of how spooked a horse could become by excessive noise.

"Go on, Isabella." Charli Sutton, lugging a tray loaded with beer mugs and whiskey shooters, grinned as Isabella passed her. "This is all for you. And let me tell you what a treat those O'Brien boys are." She winked and moved on.

"This is for me?" Isabella squeaked. "But I don't understand."

"Give the cowboys a chance to explain," Audrey said from behind her.

The aisle to the dance floor opened, giving Isabella a clear path.

Sean held Sundance's lead rope. Gabe and Tanner stood beside him. All three men were dressed in their best-pressed jeans, crisp white cotton shirts, cowboy hats and boots, and polished rodeo belt buckles. The best looking-cowboys in the whole darned place as far as Isabella was concerned.

"How did you find him?" Isabella reached out and smoothed her hand over the nervous stallion's velvety nose. She swept her fingers over the side of his neck and buried her tear-drenched face in his mane. "I can't believe you found him."

"It took some doin', but we did," Gabe said.

She pulled away from the horse and faced the men. "Why?"

"From what we gathered," Gabe nodded toward his brothers, "Sundance means a lot to you."

"We want you to continue on as his trainer." Sean stepped forward, offering her the lead.

"At the Rockin' O Ranch," Tanner added.

"Yeah, it's a bribe." Gabe smiled.

Isabella took the lead rope, her head swinging side to side. "I have money. I can pay you for him." She snorted softly. "It's O'Brien money anyway."

"The horse isn't for sale." Gabe held out his hand for Isabella's. "We want you to come with him. He obviously loves you as much as you love him."

Adding emphasis, Sundance nudged Isabella's arm.

"I can be Sundance's trainer?"

"Yeah, you don't have to work here at the Ugly Stick if you don't want to." Sean smiled. "Although it would be okay with us if you still did."

Isabella cast a glance at her boss. "I kinda got used to it."

"I'd love if you could help out during the busy times," Audrey offered. "But I'd completely understand if you quit altogether." She grinned. "You'll be pretty busy at the ranch."

Her gaze met Tanner's. "I'd want to help out with all the animals and work."

"That's what we love about you, Isabella." Tanner gave her one of his rare smiles.

She soothed a hand over Sundance's nose, handing the lead to Gabe, her heart breaking. "I can't. I'd feel like a charity case."

"Not at all, sweetheart." Sean elbowed Gabe. "Tell her the rest."

Gabe dug in his pocket and pulled out a small black jewelry box.

Isabella's eyes narrowed and she shook her head.

Gabe dropped to one knee. "Isabella Severs, Sean, Tanner and I promise to love, honor and cherish you for the rest of our lives. In return, we just want you to be a part of ours. Please, will you marry me?"

Isabella blinked. "But what if I don't want a traditional life?"

"We want to provide for you and make sure you're taken care of should anything happen to one or all of us," Gabe insisted.

With Gabe at her feet, offering her the world, all Isabella's dreams were within reach, but she was afraid it was all still a dream. "What about your father? Won't he be disappointed?"

Jonathon O'Brian cleared his throat and stepped up beside Isabella. "I'd be proud to have you as a daughter-in-law." His chest puffed out and he smiled. "I picked you for the bachelor party for a reason. And darned if my boys didn't all fall in love with you. I'm happy if they're happy."

"Any other objections?" Gabe asked. "Gettin' a little cramped down here."

Isabella's head spun and her knees wobbled. "I don't know what to say."

Tanner removed his cowboy hat and pressed it to his heart. "All you gotta do is say yes."

Sean's brows dipped. "You do love us, don't you?"

A laugh bubbled up Isabella's throat. "More than life."

"Then what are you waiting for?" Audrey piped in.

"Yes!" Isabella pulled Gabe to a standing position and wrapped her arms around his neck. "Yes. I'll marry you."

Gabe whispered into her ear. "You do realize you get three grooms for the price of one wedding ring, don't you?"

Her eyes teared up again, this time with happiness. "Yes, I do."

Tanner and Sean joined the hug.

They didn't break it up until Sundance wanted in on the action, nudging Tanner's back hard enough to make the entire group stumble.

Gabe slipped the ring on Isabella's finger. "We better get Sundance outta here before he gets antsy."

"Good idea." Audrey nodded toward the business end of the horse. "Do it before he leaves a present."

Laughter rose from the crowd of well-wishers.

Isabella led the horse out the front entrance and around to the back where they'd hidden the horse trailer. For a long moment, she hugged Sundance, talking to him softly, reassuring him that she'd never let him go again. She loaded him in the trailer, unable to believe her life had just turned a one-eighty.

Once they had the horse settled, Gabe pulled Isabella into his arms and kissed her soundly. When he came up for air, he stepped aside.

Tanner smoothed a hand along the side of Isabella's cheek. "I promise to do everything in my power to make you happy." He kissed her gently, his tongue delving past her teeth to swirl around hers.

Isabella's heart melted all over again at the tenderness the gruff cowboy was capable of. She kissed him back, loving the way he held her.

When Tanner released her, Sean swept her off her feet and danced around the parking lot, whooping. "We're gonna have a great life. Just you wait and see." He smacked a kiss on her cheek and a more passionate one on her lips, then he set her on her feet. "Where to?"

Breathless, her heart racing with the excitement of her engagement to the three strong cowboys, Isabella could think of only one place she'd rather be. "Anyone up for a little skinny-dippin' in the moonlight?"

"Sweetheart, you're makin' a habit of it. Not that I'm complaining." Gabe lifted her into his arms and strode the length of the horse trailer to his truck, depositing her in the passenger seat with a kiss to the end of her nose.

Half an hour later, Isabella and Gabe settled Sundance into his new home in the Rockin' O Ranch horse barn.

Sean led Stormy and his own gelding out of their stalls and slipped bridles over their heads.

Tanner readied his mare and Gabe's stallion.

As a full moon made a grand ascent into the night sky, Isabella and her three men rode out across the grasslands, bareback and in love.

She let her horse have her head, galloping over the rolling terrain. Isabella threw back her head and laughed, breathing in the warm Texas air, the scents of hay, horse and dust more familiar and reassuring than the beer and whiskey of the Ugly Stick.

As she neared the creek, she slowed Stormy to a sedate walk, admiring the way the moon reflected off the still waters.

Sean rode up on her left. "Have you thought about when you want to get hitched?"

"No, I haven't," she admitted. "Too much has happened for me to wrap my head around everything."

Tanner frowned. "The sooner the better."

"Don't pressure her." Gabe rode on her right. "We'll want to renovate the old homestead for a place to live. That'll take time."

"Too damned much time," Tanner groused. "I want her living with us now."

Gabe sat up straighter. "We all do. But to be fair to Isabella, she gets to decide."

Isabella laughed out loud as she reined in her horse on the banks of the creek. "I don't care. Today, tomorrow, next week… I want to be with all of you too. And like Tanner said, the sooner the better."

Tanner dropped to the ground and reached up to help her down.

Isabella slid along his long, lean body, her pussy rubbing across the ridge of his fly. When her boots touched the ground, her pulse quickened, the promise of more to come setting her body on fire. "You're overdressed," she whispered. "Let me remedy that." Her fingers loosened the buttons on his shirt, dragging the hem from his waistband.

Gabe and Sean busied themselves tying the horses to the nearby bushes.

Once she had the shirt open, Isabella smoothed her hands over Tanner's chest, shoving the shirt back over his shoulders until it slid down his arms, dropping to his feet.

She reached for his belt buckle, loosening it so that she could unbutton his jeans. Ever so slowly, she eased his zipper down, dragging out the moment with wicked intensity.

"You're killing me." He grabbed her hands, shoving them away. In seconds he'd toed off his boots, dropped his jeans and stood naked in front of her. "Now let me help you."

"I'll help." Gabe strode forward as naked as Tanner.

"Me too." Sean, his nude body glowing blue in the moonlight, hurried into the fray, grabbing her around the middle and swinging her feet into the air. "Someone get the boots."

Isabella laughed breathlessly as Gabe grabbed her boots and yanked them off.

Tanner unbuttoned her shorts and tugged them and the thong over her thighs, stopping to finger her pussy, testing its wetness. "I'm going to come before we get her completely naked."

Sean set her on her bare feet and lifted the hem of her blouse, raising it up over her head, tossing it to the side. "I get her first this time." He turned her in his arms. Bending, he lifted her, settling her legs around his hips. "Wet or dry?"

"Dry first." She nodded toward the huge, stony ledge. "I want to make love to all of you at the same time."

"Oh, baby, and we want that." Sean carried her to the stone and eased her onto her back.

He cupped her cheeks and kissed her, then moved down her body, tonguing her skin, nipping her nipples and spreading kisses all the way across her belly and lower.

Heat burned beneath every touch of his lips and fingers, building at her core and spreading outward. "More, please," she moaned.

Sean spread her thighs and lay down between them, his fingers parting her folds, his tongue finding her special nubbin of desire.

Gabe settled on her right, Tanner on her left, each

claiming a breast, their fingers massaging and tweaking the nipples, leaving Sean to do his thing.

The youngest of her O'Brien brothers slid his tongue into her pussy, circling her entrance, then sliding upward to flick her clit. He poked a calloused finger into her cunt, then two, then three, the coarseness setting off bursts of flames inside her.

Isabella's heels pressed against the stone, her back arching upward. "Oh, God, yes." Sean's relentless assault drove her up over the edge and she free-fell into an abyss of molten heat.

Sean climbed up her body and drove into her in one long, steady thrust, filling her to full and then some. Whether he had the biggest dick wasn't a factor. What he did with it extended her orgasm through his own.

When he sagged against her, he sucked in a deep breath. "You're so beautiful. I could stay like this all night."

"No way." Tanner nudged him. "Let me show her how it's done."

"I don't know…" Isabella sighed and sat up. "Sean was pretty incredible."

Sean moved to the side and Tanner hovered over her. "I have a year on him. I know a few things."

Sean chuckled. "We're talking about pleasing our woman, not breeding cows."

Tanner shot a narrow-eyed look at his brother. "Shut up and learn something."

Isabella rolled to the side, grabbed Gabe's hand, dragging herself and him to their feet. "While you two argue, we're going for a swim." She jumped into the water.

Gabe landed beside her.

When they surfaced, two more splashes drenched them all over again.

"Promise me something," she said as they all stood in water up to their waists.

"Anything." Gabe cupped her chin.

"Name it." Sean caressed her breast.

"Promise you what, baby?" Tanner lifted her left hand and pressed a kiss to her palm.

"That you'll never let me come between you."

Gabe hooked her elbow. "I don't know. Kinda have to sometimes to get this close." He pulled her against his erection.

"You know what I mean." Her right hand slipped below the surface and wrapped around his cock.

"I promise," Sean said.

"I promise," Gabe echoed.

Tanner hesitated.

Isabella pulled her left hand free of Tanner's grip and let it fall beneath the water to circle his dick. "Promise, Tanner?"

"When you put it like that..." He sucked in a deep breath and let it out in a whoosh. "I promise."

"Then let's get this party started." Isabella slid her leg along Gabe's, floating up to where her pussy hovered over his cock. "I could use a little help, Tanner."

Tanner waded behind her and gripped her waist, positioning his dick at the tight little hole of her anus.

"Sean?" Isabella reached out and tugged the man over, pressing his hand to her breast. "Now, this is what I call *the works*. I love you guys just the way you are. Don't ever change."

"Now, that I can promise." Tanner slid the tip of his dick into her ass.

Gabe entered her pussy in a long, slow glide.

Sean caressed her breast, tweaking the nipple.

The moon shone down on them, bathing them in a soft, blue glow.

Life didn't get any better than that.

As the men moved inside of her, Isabella was proved wrong.

Oh, yes it did get better…much better.

**If you enjoyed this book, try the other books in the
Ugly Stick Saloon Series**

Boots & Chaps (#1)
Boots & Sex Ed (#2)
Boots & Leather (#3)
Boots & Promises (#4)
Boots & Bareback (#5)
Boots & Dirty Tricks (#6)
Boots & Lace (#7)
Boots & Roses (#8)
Boots & Buckles (#9)
Boots & the Wishes (#10)
Boots & Twisters (#11)
Boots & the Bachelor (#12)
Boots & the Rogue (#13)
Boots & the Heartbreaker (#14)
Boots & Wings (#15)

BOOTS & DIRTY TRICKS

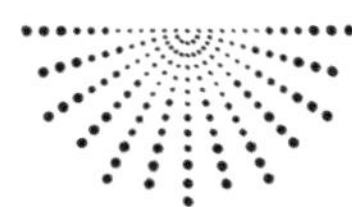

UGLY STICK SALOON SERIES #6

New York Times & USA Today
Bestselling Author

ELLE JAMES

writing as

MYLA JACKSON

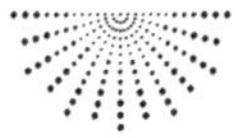

Charli Sutton sighed and swiped the surface of the bar, her hand moving in slow, listless circles, her gaze following Kendall Mason and Ed Judson as they spun and laughed around the dance floor.

"What's wrong, Charli?" Audrey, the owner of the Ugly Stick Saloon, relieved Charli of the rag and tossed it into the sink behind the counter. "You haven't been yourself lately."

"I don't know." Charli heaved another sigh. "I think I'm missing Austin." She filled an order for a cowboy in a black T-shirt, sitting at a barstool and turned back to Audrey.

Audrey shook her head. "I don't miss Austin. That's where Randy and Jason live. I've never been happier getting as far away from the city as I could."

"Yeah, I don't miss them, but I miss the nightlife and the variety of people you met there. I've been here with you at the Ugly Stick from the start, but I'm...well..." She flung her hand in the air. "I don't know."

"Bored? Lonely? Need to get laid?" Audrey chuckled. "I can understand that. Been feeling a little that way myself."

"You?" Charli blinked hard and stared at her boss, noting the beautiful strawberry blond hair and light blue eyes. "How could you be bored or lonely? You're gorgeous."

"And driven to make this place work. I don't have time to date. But you," she waived a hand in her direction, "have no excuse. You should be out there dating."

"Yeah, but it's been so long, what do I do? I'm starting to feel itchy. Wanderlust is tugging at me, making me want to leave or do something different." Charli pulled a beer mug from the shelf above her and filled it halfway from the tap, swallowing a healthy slug before she set it on the counter. The cool beer slid down her throat but did nothing to take the edge off her twitchiness.

"Are you unhappy being the assistant manager of the Ugly Stick?" Audrey asked.

"No, don't get me wrong." Charli leaned on the counter and sighed again. "I love my job."

Libby Hammons, with silky brown hair and deep cleavage flashing out of her low-cut blouse, slid her tray on the bar and offloaded the empties.

Even Libby managed to find dates in this little corner of Texas.

"Need 5 whiskey shooters, you choose the whiskey, a pitcher of Bud Light, a fruity wine cooler and five mugs for table twelve." She pushed her curly blond hair behind her ears and glanced over at Audrey. "I could use a hand with the tables in the far corner. Tia picked a bad night to be sick."

"I'll take care of them." Audrey grabbed an empty tray and hurried to the corner where the waiting customers were getting restless.

After Charli filled Libby's order and sent her on her way, she sighed for the hundredth time and slumped a hip against the bar.

"That's a mighty big sigh for such a pretty little lady."

Charli glanced at the man sliding onto the stool to her left. "What can I get you?"

"Guinness." He leaned both elbows on the counter, the movement stretching his blue chambray shirt over broad shoulders.

A tug of latent awareness pulled at Charli's gut. "Need a mug?"

"No, I like it straight from the bottle."

That tug blossomed into full-fledged attraction—the first she'd felt for a male in at least four months. Charli popped the top off the bottle and plunked it on the counter in front of the stranger. "You're not from around here, are you?"

"Actually, I am." He downed a healthy swallow and turned halfway around to watch the crowd on the dance floor.

Charli's brows dipped. "I haven't seen you in the saloon."

"Just back from a tour in Afghanistan. Before that, I was too busy preparing for deployment to stop in."

"Oh." Charli's interest perked and she looked closer. She should have known he was in the service. Hair cut short on the sides, his face angular, tanned and lean, the man reeked of military, his movements confident, strong and proud. Not a bad looking guy.

He faced her again, a smile lifting his lips, his teeth shining white in the semi-darkness of the saloon. "I'm Connor Mason, Kendall's older brother." He held out his hand.

Her brows lifted and she shook the man's hand, a jolt of awareness shimmying through her body. "Ah yes, Kendall talks about you all the time. Nice to finally meet you."

"I couldn't help but overhear your conversation with Audrey."

"It's nothin'". Charli shrugged. "I like moving around. I grew up in a family that moved every two years. I'm hitting the two-year mark here."

"Thinkin' about leavin' then?" He swirled the beer in the bottle of Guinness, his attention there.

Not on Charli, as if he didn't really care what her answer was. A stab of disappointment made her reply short, "Yeah. I think so."

His chin came up and his lips twisted. "Be a cryin' shame. I was hoping to get to know you. To me, you're a fresh face to Hole In The Wall, Texas."

"Thanks, but I live in Temptation." The blue funk she was in lifted slightly, a glimmer of hope making her smile.

The cowboy in the black T-shirt lifted a finger to capture her attention. "Can I get another beer?"

Charli hurried toward him, anxious to take care of his order and get back to her conversation with Connor. "Another draft?"

"Yes, ma'am." His lips quirked up on the ends.

After filling his order, Charli hurried back Kendall's brother. She could imagine him in a uniform, her body warming all over. She loved a man in uniform. "How do people deal with nothing to do?"

"There's always something to do around here, you just gotta know how to make things happen."

"Maybe that's my problem. I don't know how." But she'd like it if he gave her a few ideas. She looked at him from beneath her eyelashes.

"You city folks are used to having everything at your fingertips."

"Are you slamming me for being a city girl?"

"No, not at all, just makin' a statement." He leaned forward, his lips turned up at one corner. "Out here, you gotta make your own fun."

"How?" Charli flung both hands in the air. "When people leave here, they go home. The Ugly Stick is where they go to make things happen. I work here. It's not the same."

Mason shrugged and took a long pull from his beer before he answered. "Guess it's up to you to figure out what's fun." He stood, slapped a couple bills on the counter, and tipped his fingers at her. "Nice to meet you," he said in his smooth southern drawl. Then he winked, nodded to the man in the black T-shirt, turned and left the bar.

Charli couldn't take her gaze off the man. Not until he disappeared through the entrance of the saloon did she realize her heartbeat had kicked up a notch. Not only that but she hadn't sighed in the past ten minutes, nor did she feel like it.

Connor Mason had her blood pumping like no other man had in the past two years since she'd been working the Ugly Stick.

With a lift in her step, she finished her shift, helped shut down the bar, slid into her black Mustang and pulled out of the parking lot. She lifted the hair from the back of her neck and let it fly in the wind from the open window. Before she'd gone more than thirty yards down the road, her cell phone rang on the seat beside her.

Now who the hell was calling her at three o'clock in the morning?

She glanced at the caller ID.

Blocked Sender.

She debated not answering, but after the fourth ring, she hit the talk button. "This is Charli."

"Ever skinny dipped in someone else's pool?"

Deep and masculine, the voice in the receiver was the kind that made coffee commercials sound sexy. It reached out to caress Charli's ear and other more easily aroused places of her body. A shiver of awareness snaked across her skin. "Who is this?"

"Let's just say I overheard your conversation at the bar."

Her breath catching in her throat, Charli clutched the phone tighter.

"You can spice things up if you dare," he said, his voice a sensuous whisper.

Charli tried hard to think who had been sitting at the bar that evening, only conjuring one image. That of the sexy soldier who'd blatantly eavesdropped on her conversation with Audrey. "Connor?"

"I'm not tellin'."

A surge of anger spiked her adrenaline. "Look, I don't need a pervert daring me to skinny dip in someone else's pool. Do me a favor and don't call this number again."

"With a body as beautiful as yours, I'm surprised you're afraid."

Charli's thumb hovered over the off button, but the deep timbre of his voice had her mesmerized, her body heating at the rich tone. "I'm not afraid. I'm just not stupid." She'd hoped to come off indignant, but the best she could do was breathless.

"Suit yourself and play it safe...or take the dare. Judge Stephen's pool, three fifteen—be there. I'll be watching."

A click followed by silence indicated he'd hung up. Charli stared down at the phone, not sure if she'd heard things. She shook her head. No, she had not just had a call from a sexy stranger daring her to skinny dip in the judge's pool. Temptation was too small a town. Getting caught wasn't a question. Everyone was always in everyone else's business. Besides, the judge lived smack-dab in the oldest neighborhood, surrounded by old biddies who spread gossip faster than a wildfire during a long Texas drought.

What was she even thinking about this challenge for anyway?

As her SUV drove past the turn to Judge Stephen's house, her foot slipped off the accelerator, her belly tightening.

She glanced at the clock on her dash. At three-twelve

in the morning, all those old biddies were sound asleep. The judge would be as well. Her skin felt sticky from eight hours of work behind the bar and the hot Texas night wasn't helping to cool her. The thought of slipping naked into the cool waters of a swimming pool made her body yearn.

Before she could think a rational thought, her foot hit the brake, she spun the steering wheel and she slammed the accelerator to the floor, headed for the center of town. Two minutes until three-fifteen.

Mr. Sexy-Voice would be there watching.

ABOUT THE AUTHOR

Twenty years of livin' and lovin' on a South Texas ranch raising horses, cattle, goats, ostriches and emus left an indelible impression on Myla Jackson, one she likes to instill in her red-hot stories. Myla pens wildly sexy, fun adventures of all genres including historical westerns, medieval tales, romantic suspense, contemporary romance and paranormal beasties of all shapes and sexy sizes. She lives in the tree-covered hills of Northwest Arkansas with her husband of more than 20 years and her muses—the human-wanna-be canines—Chewy and Sweetpea.

To learn more about Myla Jackson and her alter ego Elle James visit:

www.mylajackson.com

mylajackson@mylajackson.com

Ugly Stick Saloon Series

Boots & Chaps (#1)

Boots & Sex Ed (#2)

Boots & Leather (#3)

Boots & Promises (#4)

Boots & Bareback (#5)

Boots & Dirty Tricks (#6)

Boots & Lace (#7)

Boots & Roses (#8)

Boots & Buckles (#9)

Boots & the Wishes (#10)

Boots & Twisters (#11)

Boots & the Bachelor (#12)

Boots & the Rogue (#13)

Boots & the Heartbreaker (#14)

Boots & Wings (#15)

Bound & Tied Series

Honor Bound (#1)

Duty Bound (#2)

River Bound (#3)

Paranormal

Shewolf (#1)

Thorn's Kiss (#2)

Sex, Lies & Vampire Hunters

Witch's Curse